I0621507

THROWING CAUTION TO THE WIND

A Third Age Writers' Perspective

A collection of works
Bryan (J.B.E.) McNally Editor

Whittlesea University of the Third Age (WU3A)
Creative Writing Group

Published by: Whittlesea U3A

Whittlesea, Victoria

Publisher:
Whittlesea University of the Third Age (WU3A)
34 Robert Street
Lalor, VIC, 3075.
https://whittleseau3a.org.au/

Cover Design by Jan Marshall and Bryan McNally
Book Layout Template © 2017 BookDesignTemplates.com

Dedicated to all of us who may have thought we were too old or set in our ways to do something different - something out there that we may have wanted to do in our younger days but didn't have the courage or time to undertake.
But now in our *third age* we blossom.

Age appears to be best in four things; old wood best to burn, old wine to drink, old friends to trust, and old authors to read.
— FRANCIS BACON

CONTENTS

Introduction

The Whittlesea University of the Third Age (WU3A) is exactly what it says. A place for learning for those who are about to enter that exciting *third age*. When you reach the *third age*, age has no boundaries. We don't stop learning just because we have left work, or our circumstances change in other ways as we grow older (and wiser).

Learning can be - new skills, hobbies that you wanted to try all your life but didn't get the time to, or just learning to make new friends with like interests and share new activities and hobbies with old friends

When I retired from work I had no idea what I was going to do. The result, a potential void, that needs to be plugged pretty quickly.

So, after a bit of post-retirement research and clues from already retired friends I checked out the WU3A and what activities were on offer. I have always wanted to write and publish my own novel and felt this would be a creative change.

In late 2016 I joined the e-Publishing class offered by the WU3A. We all thought, great, a publishing class, but what we really need is to have something to publish.

So, I decided to start a Creative Writers Group, *et voila*.

But enough about me, our boutique little group started with four participants and has grown over the past eighteen months to twelve in the class, all with different writing styles and writing objectives.

We have those who love writing fiction from historical fiction, literary fiction, science fiction and fantasy; to those who love writing memoirs, poetry and plays; to those who love writing about our beloved country and region.

We all hope you enjoy this eclectic anthology of short stories, memoirs, poems and examples of writing exercises we all performed in class.

Yours in Reading
Bryan (J.B.E.) McNally

Bev Moore

I joined WU3A and enrolled in an eBook Publishing course at the Whittlesea Community Neighborhood House. I found the course really interesting as I had written my autobiography and a manuscript on the Whittlesea Courthouse Visitor Information Centre. Our E Publishing class consisted of around 10 members but grew over time.

eBook publishing has over the years increased its capacity and branched out to entail new and interesting courses especially Creative Writing that I joined earlier this year. I have submitted various stories from my autobiography and received helpful advice and guidance with the editing of same.

I hope to submit my chapter on Ayers Rock and also other stories that I am encouraged to write in Creative Writing Class.

Dollars from Heaven - The Angel on My Shoulder

Memoir

I walked, feeling numb, a sense of hopelessness. Tears streaming down my face I walked with the wind in my face down busy High Street, in Epping. It was a bitterly cold day with an icy wind and I was walking to nowhere in particular, just a walk to get my head around what was to occur tomorrow.

My treasured friend Barbara had passed away with cancer and her funeral was the next day. But I had no money in my purse, and not enough petrol in my car to drive to Fawkner.

Gazing up at the heavens I uttered I am sorry Barb, but I am not able to say goodbye to you tomorrow, I have no money and feel so helpless.

Within seconds of those words I felt something brush my foot and looking down I saw a twenty dollar note. Blinking fast, I stooped down and retrieved the note that held firm against my shoe and holding my breath I turned around to look behind me, fully expecting someone rushing to claim my find. But there was nobody in sight. I stood still then glancing up to the sky, but this time with a smile as I whispered, "thanks Barb". How elevated I felt, in the middle of a busy street, with no money and suddenly I was, in my opinion, rich. I could put petrol in my car, but most important of all I could buy a rose to put on her coffin.

On this cold blustery day now, I knew where I was walking and that was to the nearest florist shop that just happened to be across the road. Yes, the money had found me on the opposite side of the florist shop...

I would like a special rose to put on my friends coffin I blurted out as emotion overtook me in the shop, the shop attendant nodded. "this is the best one I have" and yes it was.

The following chapter entails the written letter that I penned the night of her funeral. It was hard to write but I had to put it into words. She was my lifelong friend and there would never ever be another to replace her. Overbearing at times she could be, and bossy as well, but always her best interests were at heart and that was me. When I had to sell my house due to the disastrous Government loan scheme that saw thousands of first home buyers, in the same predicament of despair, Barb was there for me even as her health failed she stood beside me and supported me with her food hamper. When the house was sold it was Barb who arranged the truck that belonged to her brother-in-law and although it was small, I managed to squeeze everything in. I tried to express my thanks to her, but she just shrugged it off "that's what good friends do Bubbly" (her nick name for me).

The service was held at Fawkner Cemetery and as I walked towards the Chapel I heard the sounds of an engine and turning I faced the hearse that contained the body of my dear friend. Trust me, to get in the way I am sure she would have been smiling out at my look of utter shock as I stood stock still holding the rose within the cylinder tied with red ribbon.

I sat up the back listening to the Eulogy read by the Minister, her husband, then his sister. My beautiful friend gone. How could I fill the void that I knew was unfillable? After hugging her brother Reg and sister in law Carol, I had to leave, it was too hard to stand around and know she would never be in my life again.

Yet I left with the knowledge that she was there when I needed her, even in death, for she was the angel on my shoulder who arranged a cash payment for her friend ...

My WU3A Christmas 2017 - Taking A Short Cut

Memoir

Christmas 2017, the year almost at an end and I was looking forward to meeting up with my WU3A friends for our Christmas party at Manor On High in High Street Epping.

As I resided in the township of Whittlesea, I decided that having already made arrangements for my return home on the day I would travel to the venue by public transport. I would take a bus to South Morang Station and board another bus to Epping where I would alight at the Epping shopping center and, just a short walk, or at least I thought, to the happy event.

The bus driver on the Epping run was extremely chatty and he asked where I was off to and I told him Manor On High. I added that I was getting off at Epping Plaza.... "Oh, I know a short cut he told me, instead of going to Epping Plaza, get off at Northern Hospital and walk through their car park at the rear of the hospital"

Goody thought I, even better as I had chosen a new pair of shoes that had not been previously worn in.

After alighting from the bus and waving to the friendly driver, I headed in the direction of what I thought would be the rear car park.

But somehow after walking for ten minutes or so I found myself in a vast open area that resembled a development of some kind, but without any cars, the entire area was empty... Where am I - I thought? I kept walking and noted how large industrial trucks were appearing at intermittent intervals and seemed to be staring at me with a puzzled look.

My feet were hurting as I walked on and I felt stressed and confused as the sight of busy High Street seemed to be avoiding me.

Finally, I saw traffic up ahead and so I walked in the direction and reached High Street where I stood still to try to get my bearings. Then I heard the whir of a motor bike and it was a smiling Australia Post lady who asked me "Are you Ok Love – what are you looking for? Feeling relieved at last help was at hand, I replied, "Manor On High" Still smiling widely she pointed in the opposite direction that I had been facing prior to her arrival.... "there it is over there just past that sign"

I thanked her and feeling elated I continued to the Manor On High to meet up with all my WU3A friends.

It was as always and typical of a social WU3A event, a memorable afternoon, however I was in a great deal of discomfort due to blisters that had formed across both heels of my feet. With smiles and waves I watched my line dancing class enjoying themselves but also dancing to perfection. Some of them beckoned to me to join in but I shook my head and pointed to my feet. I had longed to join in but simply put, my feet could not handle the movements after my "short cut"

So there were, I knew, certain tables that I did not get to visit and dances that I had missed out on, so I promised myself to make up for it at the 2018 WU3A Manor On High Christmas party.

No more short cuts across a car park that was in fact, as I learnt later, COSTCO parking facilities and access points...

This year I am going in style **TAXI**....

The Filing Compactus –
If Only...

Memoir

During my employment with a well-known Superannuation Firm in the outer CBD area, I had formed a close bond with my colleagues both in the Melbourne and Sydney Head Office.

In my role as administration officer it was part of my duties to update and assist with the data entry of company file client information and also send requested files to Sydney in the overnight mail bag.

However, as time passed the both offices would undergo a restructure and head office informed it had the required space to finally house the client files of just over 3,0000 and take over the administration from the Melbourne based team.

The Melbourne Admin team including myself were redeployed into other areas within the company, mine being the mail room.

I took the opportunity to ask my supervisor if I may be able to assist in the packing and shipment of the files, when the time arrived to them to travel. However, my request was denied, and I was informed that temporary staff would be employed to undertake the packaging of the files. I was disappointed but accepted that decision...

Over the next week temporary staff were hired to pack the files into boxes and they were hard workers indeed. On the Friday with their job done they were thanked and sent on their way.

All that was left was the pick up by the freight carrier to ship the boxes to Tullamarine for their flight to Sydney Head Office located in the CBD.

As I went about my mail room duties the following Monday afternoon, I received a phone call from one of my Sydney colleagues.... "Hi Bev" she said " I cannot find Mr. Alberton (not his real name) Our boxes got a bit waterlogged due to the heavy storms over the weekend and the basement is a bit flooded at this time but I managed to get to box A and he is not in it"   I assured her, after checking with my ex administration boss, that all files were returned to the compactus for shipment to Sydney.

On Tuesday morning I was paged to the phone and again it was one of the Sydney admin team, "Bev we cannot find any of the files in the boxes they are supposed to be in – we checked the alpha status and the files seem to be out of order" I sensed the dirty look portrayed by the bossy overbearing supervisor, who seemed to be under the impression I was on a personal call, so I waited till my Sydney colleague had finished her sentence before asking her if she would like to speak to the mail room supervisor, and her reply was short "No thanks Bev Take care" and with that she hung up.

 As I returned to my work, I surmised that with the exit of the filing system, would possibly see changes occur in the mail room so I planned to update my resume.

I was on my morning tea break the following morning when I was paged to the phone. It was the Manager from the Taxation Area Sydney Head Office... he introduced himself and then relayed the news that over 3,000 client files had been shipped to Sydney, in alphabetical order, but under their Christian names. "How did it get to that Bev? We are pulling our hair out and the staff are under extreme pressure from the clients – Please would you be able to let me know who organized the packing of the files. We also do not to have a list of each box content as was the instructions"

As he spoke, I recalled the first day when the temps were given the instructions and one of them tried to ask a question but was told to "just get on with what I have told you" As the supervisor walked off I caught him pulling a face as he whispered something to his colleague.

"If I may shed a bit of light, this list you speak of is located on our Excel Spread Sheet and gave him the file name that I had found on my computer.... "Thanks Bev and for everything you have done, the staff send their best wishes" Just a few minutes later the phone rang on the supervisors desk and as she introduced herself I heard the irate tones of the taxation manager and could hear clearly " due to your incompetence our company are facing a crisis" and on it went as I continued to sort through the stack of "Return To Sender" envelopes and thinking to myself , if only.

Bryan McNally

Bryan McNally is an exciting new author whose subject matter transcends mainstream and edge taking thrills.

Bryan has vast experience in all forms of writing in his roles within industry and has taken these skills along with his energetic imagination to produce works of historical fiction, memoirs, poetry and first fiction novel The Vytautas Pursuit.

His extensive travel and research landed him with the concept for The Vytautus Pursuit. In melding the intense and varied history of Lithuania and its forefathers with daring concepts and linkages throughout

His second Jack Carpenter novel, *The Eriksson Bequest*, is coming soon and mixes the splendour of Iceland with intrigue on both sides of the law.

In addition to being author of the Jack Carpenter Novels, Bryan leads a Creative Writing Group at the Whittlesea U3A in Melbourne.

Connect with Jack and J.B.E

Check out my website: http://theadventuresofjackcarpenter.com/
Subscribe to my Blog: http://theadventuresofjackcarpenter.com/blog
Email me: jbemcnally@theadventuresofjackcarpenter.com
Follow me on Twitter: @knackerzzz
Friend Me on Facebook: https://www.facebook.com/knackerzz
Friend Jack on Facebook: https://www.facebook.com/AdventuresofJack-Carpenter/

Andrew Barton (Banjo) Patterson

Narrative Essay

Given my love of writing and tireless aim to be the best I can, I recall one of my lecturers on a writing course saying;

'If you aspire to writing fiction or non-fiction at a specific literary level, read classic poetry at the same level and you *will* achieve your desires.'

So where should I begin? Keats? Wordsworth? Shelley? All great poets, but did they ever define the culture of their home countries? Some would say they achieved claims to certain niches of their ways of life, but none could say their works defined their homelands pioneer life as did the person I would give my right arm to go back in time and not only meet but have a long chat to. Absorb the inspiration first hand from someone who could make you feel you were right there in the midst of Australia's pioneers as they grew and developed our great country.

Banjo Patterson was born at 'Narrambla", near Orange NSW. What a coincidence! I would not have had this life if not for Glenise's cousin, Jeannette, from Orange hadn't introduced us at a St Valentine's Day party 44 years ago. We are all still close and visit often.

About two years ago it was our turn to visit Jeannette in Orange and she said, "Why don't we do something a little different and visit some of Orange's cultural gems?"

Mount Canobolis and the views over the old and newer parts of the City. Some classic wineries. Gulgong home of Henry Lawson and finally, Banjo Patterson's cottage, Narrambla, relocated to the heart of Orange so locals and visitors alike could marvel at the life of a cultural genius.

I couldn't believe it as I walked through the front door to this amazing slice of history. My mind started to wander as I placed myself back in time to the late 1800s talking to Banjo as if he were my best mate

"Banjo, how does it feel to have created the greatest ballad of all time, the defining moments of Australia's life in the outback, an anthem that wasn't, but should have been?" My love of the many renditions of Waltzing Matilda spinning around in my mind as I posed my first question. Tom Waits with his sandpaper voice, evincing emotions from deep within, all of those Grand Finals that the Magpies played in (and lost) that were headlined by great Aussie artists chanting in time with the crowds, our spurned *true national anthem* rendering God Save the Queen a long second as an opening interlude to these special events.

"Well Bryan, believe it or not Waltzing Matilda has some very unusual origins." Banjo had me spellbound as he continued. "My love for travelling on foot and wandering our stunning burnished landscape meant I wanted to reflect that in its title and chorus. Waltzing was an easy choice. From the German auf der Walz, 'on the roll', best described my creative years and how I got to see the many and varied vistas of our great land.

"You might be forgiven for thinking that Matilda was my bride with whom I go waltzing. But it's not. Not yet anyway. I hadn't met Alice back then only after my wanderings brought me back closer to home. A matilda is an old slang term for swag, where you keep all of your essential belongings that you might need on your travels. So there I was travelling around my land with my belongings in my swag - '*Waltzing Matilda.*'" Banjo's explanation was full of joy but I had to ask him why such a tragic ending to the work.

"Banjo, why such a sad ending to such a beautiful story? Surely the squatter could afford one measly jumbuck for the poorly swagman?" Banjo, with some melancholy in his voice came back to me as he led me through the reception room of his old cottage, down the hallway and into his den, where many of his classic works were born.

"Bryan, back in the day everyone had to earn their keep. Nobody got *nuthin fur nuthin*," Banjo explained in his Colonial Aussie dialect. "The squatters earned their land and considered the swagman should earn his chattels also. It was what it was lad. My writing reflects the real Australia, not how we would all like it to be"

As we sat down in Banjo's study, I reflected on his many classic works and how my curiosity should be manifested next in this brief, surreal meeting with this one-in-a-hundred-year prodigy of Australian and world literature.

"'AB', if I may call you that?" My mind went through all of those priceless works of his, The man from Snowy River, Clancy of the Overflow, The Geebung Polo Club, Saltbush Bill. There were too many to have him share his reminiscences of all with me, so I took the best of all worlds. "AB, apart from Waltzing Matilda what is your favourite? I love them all, they send me into a transcendental state of relaxation, my mind floating back in time at the way things were and how the obstacles that our pioneers encountered would have been near impossible to overcome."

"What a great question lad," was his lingering reply as he framed his thoughts to give me his true philosophy of the bygone days of Australian life.

"You see they all tell roughly the same story, and as such, they are all my favourites - all first amongst equals."

"The Man from Snowy River tells the tale of freedom through the eyes of the progeny of a champion racehorse who escapes to run wild with the brumbies of the outback.

"Clancy of the Overflow shows how the stifling life of a city dweller yearns and envies the life of Clancy, an itinerant shearer and drover working at the Overflow station. The suppression of the city for the freedom of the drover's life.

"Saltbush Bill is a freewheeling sheep drover who fought tooth and nail to have his sheep roam freely as they converged on the station. Bill knew his sheep as his extended family, their freedom his only objective before they reached their inevitable end."

"You see, Bryan, that's what it was all about. Our vibrant young countrymen and women were so in need of inspiration to follow their free spirit. My course was well set in my writings to inspire and hail our beloved pioneers."

As I sipped the Billy Tea that Jeannette passed to me from the woodfired stove I couldn't help but reflect that Banjo's revered writings way back when, and their messages, were no different to today as Australia fights for equality and freedom for its youth and the prosperity of tomorrow.

The Storm Wasn't Forecast!

Essay

We had been sweltering with the incessant heat from the corona of our closest star, our life blood without which we couldn't survive. Nearly one hundred and fifty million kilometres from us, passing across a plethora of atmospheric layers, its ferocity not diminished by the dilution on its way through.

This has been one of the most severe Melbourne Summer's. Forty-nine days without rain. Every day I strap on the *Nikes,* throw on the lycra shorts and top and head out for my walk, just before sunrise when good old *Sol* was at its least vicious.

The ancient Egyptians worshipped her as Ra. It represented one of their many deities. Its power was boundless, providing energy, conditions by which we could see each other, our reflections gave thanks to the sun in making all things visual possible. We couldn't live without it.

But this summer was atypically sultry.

Out the door I go, fiftieth day without rain, *Ra* about to poke its visage above the low-rise landscape of Bundoora as I head down the diminutive man-made valley of the University Hill wetlands. Replete with bird life, swans, ducks, purple hen and Ibis, in harmony with the frogs their symphony was something to behold. Then back up to street level to make my way to the Plenty Gorge Park, whistling a somewhat less harmonious tune attempting to resonate in time with the *locals.*

The gorge, haven for much wildlife, kangaroos, wombats, all types of *nasty* reptiles, tiger, brown and black - all willing to mind their own business until trodden on, so beware behind the beauty hides the beast.

Each day came and went and still no break in the weather, although the BOM would have you believe they were Sports Bet, giving odds each day and trying to force some rain with their specious forecasts. *'Fine Until Further Notice'* should have been their catch-cry.

Still I wasn't deterred. My daily walk important to me. Like the forty-nine days before it and the forty-nine days ahead of me. I dressed for the stifling heat each day and simply ignored the predictions of the bureau.

As I descended further into the gorge, completely oblivious to the onset of the daily conditions as the Sun emerged from its slumber, I dwelt on the foliage. The superb Aussie flora that is so unique. If it wasn't for its resilience no doubt it would have succumbed by now. Even the yellow-ochre of the parched grains of grass would bounce back on a springboard of autumn rain.

As I took deep breaths passing through the densest copses of gumtrees within the gorge, the magical aroma and curative effect of the eucalyptus oil, made more potent by the heat of the morning, commenced its work on my less than perfect sinuses. I loved that freshness, that signature Australian redolence only eucalypts could deliver.

Smell not the only sense enhanced. The blue haze as you peered into the distance just ahead of this long tunnel-like copse of trees. It was something special. Like a surreal religion. Its genesis clearly one of those special days when Jesus went to work back then.

Being so caught up in the peace and the moment, I overlooked the fact that I'd been walking nearly an hour. Half past seven and still no sun. What's Old *Ra* doing? Having a sleep in?

Being so preoccupied with Mother Nature as I was, I hadn't noticed the roiling of the nimbus and cumulonimbus gloom rolling in. I wasn't going crazy. It was a cloudless sky when I left home. Same conditions for the past forty-nine days.

The distant crack of thunder that surely was the sound of lightning. Only separated by time. The time it took for its echo to reach you after the light had appeared from the bolt that had just shot from the heavens. Was Thor angry with the BOM or were we just due for a long-awaited answer to nature's prayers.

In any event, in my not-so-waterproof lycra gear I was in for a soaking on my way home. My usual pace quickened as I climbed out of the gorge. It morphed into a run as the first heavy drops started to fall. They were typical of a summer downpour, quite dispersed and the gaps were large. If I ran quick enough I reckoned I could see them missing me altogether.

But for some reason I slowed. All these days in a row I would splendour at the way nature would wake in the morning. The wildflowers opening to the sun's call. The trees aglow as their fluids warmed and they came to life. Now I had the chance to see what her reaction would be to this stark change in climate. I had almost forgotten after all this time

I could almost hear the creaking of the tree bark saying to the rain…'come on in, my capillaries need some exercise, I've been thirsty for so long.

The grass humbled by the immenseness of the gums would squeak rather than creak. You could almost picture the dead bits coming to life and new blades being born by the second

The thunder and lightning didn't ease up, nor did the rain. Heavier by the minute, I was now a sodden mess. But I didn't care. *The storm wasn't forecast*, but that made it all the more special. My stunning gorge had shed its fear of the hand it had been dealt over the summer. It didn't care so nor did I. It just bathed in the glory of rainfall. Nectar form the Gods a lifeline for one and all.

Just Another Thursday Night at Bingo

Short Story: Writing exercise to use the words 'Bingo' and 'Bikies'

The congregation was settling in at their tables, having filled their thermal mugs with International Roast or Lanchoo, depending on their penchant for either tea or coffee. Although the local RSL could barely justify calling these poor excuses for floor sweepings neither tea, nor coffee, surely.

There was Emily and Dave, Josie and Pete, Sue and Alan, Janet and Carlos, and finally Bruce and Kevin. Table 9 of the twenty tables was their weekly destination. Every Thursday night. Seven-Thirty. Right after their senior's meal, also at table 9, logistically made sense after all. No need to move too far to tackle the latest jackpot.

Ah! Bingo! The spellbinding rotation of the elliptical cage, broken only by the rasping rattle of the eighty balls bouncing and bobbing as the cage sped around clockwise and counter clockwise three times before the MC slowed it down and allowed one of the numbered spheres to escape with its life, immortalised in writing on the lucky players' cards (at least until the next game).

Sixteen times that would happen, or until some lucky punter yelled "BINGO". We were up to rotation number eight of sixteen when... No-one yelled bingo. But still the cage stopped, the balls stopped their incessant rattling and rolling and for once the MC was silenced. No legs eleven. No two fat ladies. No number nine the Brighton line. The entire RSL hall was silenced. The sipping and slurping of the thermal mugs even stopped as one.

But only the usual sounds of Bingo were silenced. The deep, low thrum. The resonance and rumble of exhaust pipes in unison. Rumble!

Rumble! Rumble! Never have these 'Senior Cits' been exposed to the temerity of any outsider interrupting the most important event in their Thursday Night calendars. Bingo!

The rumbling ceased, but this time not with the same harmonic cessation of the bingo balls. As if motors were being switched off at random. The hall was hushed. You could hear a pin drop. Not only that, but you could also hear the metal-to-bitumen scratching and scraping as the bike stands were set in place one-by-one.

Footsteps followed in sequence. Full bodied footsteps, the sound of which could only be produced by the leather riding boots of your typical Hells Angels or Comancheros bikie gang members. Clip-clop, up the RSL front steps, twenty tables, one hundred and twenty sets of eyes, all turned as one anticipating who-knows-what would emerge from the other side of the double doors representing the only barrier between the bingo-playing elderlies and whatever peril loomed just outside the portals of the hall.

All in all, there were five bikes at the foot of the steps. Engines creaking and clanking as they cooled down after their no doubt high-speed journey from who-knows-where.

The MC was holding the microphone in his left hand in anticipation of when he might get back on with the Thursday evening festivities. His other hand hovering over the green go switch of the ball tumbler. Waiting patiently for the others to refocus and for what or who were on the other side of the double doors.

The congregation gasped in harmony as the doors gently spread inwards. There was no violent shoving of the doors. No rattling of the hinges. And most importantly no-one under the age of sixty-five straddling the entry/exit threshold as they walked, and some stumbled in.

There was no barrier to age in the appreciation of beautiful machinery. The bikies who alighted their Harley-Davidsons only minutes before had been riding for an average of fifty years. They were late. Late for their once a month bingo appointment at the RSL.

The anticipation of the throng inside hadn't been based upon fear but on concern for the five riders and their pillion passengers. Tonight, like every fourth Thursday of the month, there would be twenty-one tables, NOT twenty. Tonight, the pot would be swollen by that extra table of ten. A thousand dollars instead of nine hundred. Well worth winning to every one of those one hundred and twenty, no, one hundred and thirty players.

The players breathed a sigh of relief, the MC exhaled as well, switched on his microphone and said, "It's bloody well about time, we all thought you'd been pulled over for speeding, or worse still ended up at another RSL offering more prize money."

A single voice in response reverberated from the back of the hall as they made their way to Table twenty-one, "No way, Jack, the Bikies and Bingo Clan cannot be bought! Let the cage rotate. Let the balls roll. And may lady Luck allow us, just for once to win this godforsaken prize, we're all short on petrol and our next pension check is still a week away."

All were seated as Jack bleated out the numbers with a stentorian voice, hardly needing the microphone.

" Legs eleven. Two fat ladies, eighty-eight. Number nine the Brighton line. Two little ducks, twenty-two."

"Bingo," cried Kevin on Table nine.

"Stuff it!" cried the bikies in unison on Table twenty-one.

Jack simply reset the balls and started the cage rolling once again. One hundred and thirty people. Eyes-down, obeying Jack's well-worn entreaty.

Life on a Page -
those moments in time

*"Life is not measured by the number of breaths you take, but by
the moments that take your breath away" (George Carlin).
When have you had such a moment?*
Short Story

Twenty-two times. Inhale. Exhale. Every minute of our waking and
sleeping hours. In. out. Taking over one thousand three hundred breaths
each hour, perhaps a few less as our heart slows to a crawl during our
blissful slumber overnight. Each year we will breathe in and out nearly
twelve million times, and if we all live until the ripe old average age of
eighty we will find that those precious doses of oxygen pass our lips
nearly a billion times.

You could be forgiven for thinking that I'm obsessed with counting
down my life three seconds at a time, but that couldn't be further from
the truth. Its those small, but life-changing moments that happen when
you least expect them. Those moments that give you cause to think that
you are about to lose your balance as the giddiness takes over. Those
moments that have the audacity to render you breathless, to cause you
to lose some of those *precious* one billion breaths.

But wait! I think I now know what life is all about. It *is* about those
special moments that leave you gasping for air. The peaks and troughs
that are turning points in our days on earth. What an ethereal juncture.
All of those times I have endured and experienced in my sixty-six years
on this mortal coil.

My first day of school. Mum actually paid a shilling every week to
Katie, a grade two girl to make sure I finished my lunch of vegemite
sandwiches and various pieces of fruit.

Learning to ride my bike that first time. I was nearly seven, a little late in the scheme of things. My childhood friends were way ahead and I used to get plenty of snide remarks - slowcoach, Mummy's boy, 'where's ya training wheels'. They had a Dad to expedite their pathway to bike riding. I didn't.

My first car at seventeen. A 1958 Holden Wagon. I was on top of the world. Mum never drove, so the next door neighbour kindly offered to come with us to drive it home. My first driving lesson, self-delivered, was manifested in a once vertical apricot tree tumbling to the horizontal. Minimal damage to my shiny chrome bumper bar.

My first date - breath taken away. My only girlfriend - breath taken away. The proposal - deep breaths first, then breath taken away. The long awaited answer - felt like an eternity but really only took thirty seconds - Yes, breath taken away.

Two irresistible bundles from heaven, the deepest breaths ever taken away twice within three years. And so many times over the past thirty years, countless interruptions to the normal resting heart rate breathing patterns. My boys never failed to give me cause to be proud.

Now it was sadness' time to endure. Mum losing her battle for dignity. 'I will *not* leave my home. No aged care for me.' She said through teary eyes with a croaky voice. Weeks later, with ninety-two glorious years *under her belt,* she left me an orphan. Yes, my breath taken away. One of life's troughs after so many peaks. My grief should have been manifest, but I could only recall my breath leaving with Mum's soul. No tears. No regrets. I still ponder this aberration.

So, the question, '*when have I had such a moment?*', barely possible to answer in the singular. These moments are like timelines throughout life. Things that will compress into a collage of lucid memories in those final breaths one takes. Eighty years, one billion breaths, all archived into those handful of moments that take your breath away.

✦★★૨ૉ★★✦

'Remember, the First Pancake You Make Will be Rubbish.'

Poem

Remember, the First cut is the deepest!
      The knife plunged ever deeper,
      Profound, yet more profound
      But there was no blood
      Just hurt, the worst hurt imaginable
      Life snuffed in an instant
      That lasted what seemed an eternity
      Until I was healed, or at least thought I was

Remember, First in best dressed
      And the dressings were only a band-aid treatment
      The drugs didn't help, there was no blood, remember!
      Just insufferable ringing between my ears.
      So I woke up
      Got out of bed
      Got dressed in seconds flat
      Apologies to John Lennon

Remember, First among equals
      An egalitarian society where no-one rules
      Anarchy in the UK (and everywhere else)
      Apologies to Sid Vicious
      Imagine, said Lennon (not Lenin)
      If we could all live in peace
      Black, white, yellow, red
      Who cares we all love each other

Remember, First come First served
       But that's not egalitarian
       Surely all come, all served
       But a quandary, we would need as many servers
       Which by definition,
       Would not be First among equals
       Would not be First come First served
       I think the drugs are starting to wear off, BRRR!!

Remember, the First pancake you make will be rubbish
       I now awake, begin to shake
       My first attempt at rhyme a failure
       All I need to do now is await my jailer
       Guilty! My verse could not get worse
       But wait, a cadence at last
       I surely must end this poem fast
       Over and done I get my gun, my first pancake my last

What have I gotten myself into……

Class Exercise - I woke up and to my surprise…

I woke up this morning and to my surprise, when I got myself out of bed it wasn't my bed. Had I still been in the midst of a weird dream? No! I finally remembered I had been successful in my application to be one of only ten *lucky* people to *road-test* a new style of holiday resort in Far North Queensland. Completion had only been one week earlier and on this very day the developers had only just received the occupancy certificate for the property.

The carpet smelled like freshly cultivated hay. The appliances in the common kitchen and common room had that first use smell after being fired up for breakfast. As I turned the corner from my sleeping quarters to the corridor I saw nine others milling around over the coffee pot with the same dazed and confused look I had when I first woke. Being in Unit one, I had longer to walk and I would use that as my excuse for being late.

After I bade everyone a collective good morning, my nine co-testers bade me a collective one in return, 'Good morning', they bellowed, with an attempt at being *bright-eyed and bushy tailed*, all in unison. Why did I feel the odd one out? They seemed too *together* for my liking. Had these testers been randomly selected, as was I?

With a shrug of my shoulders, I poured myself a coffee and turned to start a conversation. You know, if it's a resort, I had to be sociable. Get to know your fellow vacationer and all that. When I did so, I noticed they all wore the same clothes as me. When I dressed this morning I thought, *that's odd they even provide clothes for whatever activity this resort is into.* The gear was not exactly the height of fashion. Khaki green in colour. Short sleeve slip-on top, with matching pants. Not unlike the clobber a surgeon would wear.

When I looked closer at the rest of the testers, I noticed one major difference between them and I. They all had the same purplish-green mark at their left elbow, and a somewhat vacant stare coming from their glazed over eyes. I was unsettled!

Just as I was starting to come to grips with all of this I was snapped out of my ponderings by the opening and slamming of a very heavy metal door at the far end of the common room. In marched a foreboding figure. At least two-hundred and fifteen centimetres tall, face like nothing I had seen and growled in a guttural tone, 'Hhhhrr,' and grunted as he cleared his sandpaper throat, 'come on its your turn, you are the lucky last!!'

With that, I turned on my heels and made for the nearest exit I could find, well knowing that this *little* adventure was a long way from being over.

14th June 2017

Jovi dims the stars in moonlight debut

Short Story

My very first film after all this time singing my backside off. Platinum records. Sell out concerts. All that toil and sweat. Granted, a lucrative career and fame and relative fortune. So I spread my wings. An offer too good to refuse.

"Hey, JBJ, why don't you give yourself a challenge. Dump Jersey and come to the glitter and glitz of the big H, Hollywood awaits." David Anspaugh, lauded Hollywood Director, trying to seduce me, clearly deficiently inexperienced thespian, to "*Go East Young Man*" and dip my toe in the boiling cauldron of the celluloid heroes.

"OK", was my one word (or was it one acronym) reply, nothing more nothing less. No in-depth interrogation of what the film was all about much less its all important title. After all, I don't think David really cared if I could act my way out of a paper bag. *John Bon Jovi,* that's me and that's all he cared about. With a monumental move like this he would have bums on seats at the cinemas hanging on to the edge of their seats to either hear Bon Jovi sing his lines or see him bomb out big time in his first acting job.

I wasn't going to let either of those outcomes get anywhere near reality. I'm a proud dude and aim to excel at whatever I do. That's Show Biz, I guess.

So off I go in the winter of '95, bags packed, like a fair maiden from the prairie heading to the big city for her first job. Young and dumb and you know the rest…

With my directions in hand I make the studio on time for my first rendezvous with Anspaugh and his film crew. To my chagrin this was not going to be the one-on-one meeting I'd hoped for. The so-called briefing was one to a hundred smack in the middle of the largest tin shed I'd ever laid eyes on. Not the cramped, confined spaces of a Memphis recording studio.

So!! Down to it. Many late nights reading, reading and more reading. And then more reading; but this time back in my digs in front of the mirror. Until first rehearsal time. That's when the *ship hit the land.* Whoopi, Gwyneth, Elizabeth P and Kathleen. I was starstruck, to plagiarise an old movieland saying. Amongst all these doyens of the silver screen. I had to come back down to earth if I was going to leave an impression.

I soon did when Whoopi said, "Who the hell are you son, and how *did* you land this part?"

That was my cue to blow them all away. To prove I was worthy.

666

What made it worse, my exciting first gig was playing a house painter, contracted to maintain, but in reality, contracted to console. Pretty much everyone in the movie had been shaking off some tragedy or other and it seemed to be my mission in life to lessen the pain.

It was all about dear Rebecca, her husband taken from her prematurely and without warning. Yes, my job was to console not paint. This was a no-brainer. All of the other people in her life were dysfunctional and could barely console themselves.

666

Six months on and its opening night. No previews. No film reviews. This was a well-kept secret in most part, except for the *leaking* of the Jon Bon Jovi bit. I felt compelled to leap on to the stage in front of the screen and do a rendition of "Livin' on a Prayer". After all there was not an empty seat in the house.

The curtain came up. The opening credits rolled on. Past Whoopi. Past Gwyneth. Past all of those other household names, and there I was.

One hour and fifty minutes later the curtain descended to the unmistakeable sounds of raucous applause. I'm almost certain that those standing with their hands clapping incessantly were looking my way and I didn't even have to sing one note.

666

Morning couldn't come too quickly. Tossing and Turning all night. I leapt out of bed and headed for the door of my hotel suite. The morning papers. The movie reviews. Would they notice a little known actor, well known singer, and would they acknowledge my performance as well as I acknowledged it myself? Wishful thinking, I thought until I opened the *daily* to the entertainment section and the ever expanding grin that appeared on my face was the product of one thing and one thing alone. The one line headline about opening night of "Moonlight and Valentino"

666

Jovi dims the stars in moonlight debut

Don Langdon

Don Langdon was born in England and is socially classed, by the media pigeon holing service, as a baby boomer. After graduating from university, he has lived on three continents and worked on four. During the last three decades he spent a quarter of his time travelling the world on business.

His earlier forays into writing were technical papers, marketing blurb and a software manual.

Now he has turned his innovative scientific mind to science fiction and created the politically incorrect satire called '**Pre Dot Blue Moon**', Book 1 in the Skuide series. Book 2 in the series, '**Pre Dot New Moon**', will be available soon.

Home is Where Your Hat Is

*Writing Exercise: "It had been ten years since I had been home
and didn't know what to expect."
Short Story*

I thought I had lost it, my *hat* that is, but there it was hanging on their hall stand. It couldn't be anyone else's or could it? What do you say or do in such a situation?

I had just flown into London after a two week stint in Riyadh and was staying with my old boss Charlie and his lovely wife Cath. We hadn't seen each other in years, mostly because I had moved continents twice in that time and now resided on the other side of the globe. It was good of them to put me up for the weekend. My next stop on this tour of duty was Saint Jeoire en Faucigny for another couple of weeks work, after that I could go home to Melbourne.

The straw *hat* of Van Gogh fame hung there temptingly as I trundled my bag into their spare room. Once unpacked, I joined Cath and Charlie in their living room. After a brief chat they asked if I would like to go for a walk and feed the ducks in the park. Compared to being cooped up in a plane for hours, it sounded idyllic. The Pyrenees might be spectacular to fly over but a duck pond was friendlier and more inviting.

I went back to my room, which looked just the same as it did all those years ago when my wife and I had last come to visit them with our new little boy. Charlie's paintings hung on the walls. Many were scenes from Holland that I recognised from our Dutch sojourn twenty years ago. Where had the time flown? Shoes, hat, jacket, wallet and camera, I was all set and ready to go.

We met in the hallway. Charlie picked up the *hat* and replaced mine with it saying, "Still fits you."

Cath looked at me and said, "You left it here last time. Don't worry old big head hasn't worn it, it's too small for him."

"Dinner at the Bridge House on me," I said, as went we went out of the door laughing.

It was just like coming home.

Stalled

An Extract from the Skuide Series of books:
Novel Extract

The Skuide Stasis Watch were not concerned about individual things, but too many coincidental small things were being held in abeyance for no apparent reason. Hence they could not feel complacent about the future. The Originals had found something to interest them, thank goodness. The Blaids were on a mission which appeared to be genuine but with nasty undertones. Armaments were being bought for stockpiling. Dock, Con and Prop were on holiday with their wives, visiting Daisy's (Prop's wife) family in Tertorbia. In general, all they could conclude was that nothing untoward was showing up. Could this be the lull before the storm or was life just plodding along?

Dragoon Dragon, a Skuide Youngster of about 6 billion years of age, was currently looking after the military demands from the planet side team. He was aware that the Primeval Skuide called Miaow wanted to visit the planet again but still had not joined the covenant.

His reason being, that it was all in the past, he was just revisiting the past and it had not affected them when he and his cohort had arrived back eleven months ago. Miaow wanted to visit Twit but Dragon was not happy as he knew Twit was planning to wed the mysterious Millicent Dewdrop, yet had not actually got around to asking her, the lazy so 'n so. The only other Skuide Miaow seemed interested in visiting was Dock's friend, the frosty Ancient called Warden, who was currently a Watcher for the Blaids.

Dragon and Miaow sat in their respective spaceships glowering at one another.

Neither dared trust themselves to go to the other's ship for a meeting but someone did appear in both ships on the respective occupant's shoulder, scaring the living daylights out of them both. Nothing should have got through their shields but there was Squeaky Beak, a trans-dimensional bird-like creature with two heads. It shook both its heads in exasperation.

Squeaky Beak, in Skuide terms, is a controller and usually associated with Warden. Controllers help reduce the Skuide tendency to over react, by being so apathetic that they make doing nothing seem like an extreme measure.

"You lot make communication so difficult, why not meet on neutral territory?" sighed the diminutive Squeaky Beak. "Perhaps I can help you two boys broker a deal."

Fortunately, Squeaky Beak had the options of other dimensions to be in. An alien calling them under developed humans was tantamount to requesting euthanasia. Both Skuide vented their fury on the spaces where Squeaky Beak had been. They then looked sheepishly at one another and nodded in silent agreement, 'Stefan's, now.'

In a far off dimension very nearby, Squeaky Beak chuckled and said into a receptive ear, "Mission completed."

In all fairness, it must be pointed out that Stefan's is a relatively small crater and that Skuide spaceships are relatively large, so fitting one in is impossible and two is unthinkable. In darkside geostationary orbits, two spaceships simultaneously launched two groundcars which landed on top of Mel's atmosphere holding force field. The noise of the landing caused a break in the music. The interlude thus created, meant that Mel let them in.

Miaow called out to them as he got out of his groundcar, "Sorry to interrupt your little get together but we have to sort out a fundamental difference of opinion."

The quintet watched in trepidation as the second high noon scenario squared up, as Dragon and Miaow faced one another in that sunless crater. The Primeval Skuide opened his mouth and bleated, "Baa."

Dragon doubled up with laughter, as did the rest of the audience. Once dignity had been restored, the nosy quintet wanted to know what it was all about. The replay highlighted a problem the Stasis Watch was having and how it was beginning to effect the timeless Skuide and their impatience to get on with doing things.

"All that aside why are you lot here?" enquired Dragon.

The replay of the quintet's time spent at Stefan's did nothing to resolve the Twit and Warden dilemma for Dragon with regards to Miaow's request.

Mel was the first to speak, "I know we will not progress musically until this is resolved, so how about we have a tea break while we think of a workable solution."

All agreed to a workable solution session but eyed Mel suspiciously as he was not a renowned tea drinker. He looked at his fellow Skuide knowing what they were thinking and smiled mischievously as he remembered the formula for tiddly tea, regretting not having the ingredients at hand. Mel expanded his groundcar's dimensions to allow all seven to sit down, while he dispensed regular tea and they added whatever condiments took their fancy.

"Come on Mel, where's your manners, tea and no bikkies?" complained Judge. "Er, sorry no. I'm watching the old waistline," crooned Mel.

"Hospitality dictates..." began Judge.

"I'll get some from my supply," interjected Jester and skipped out for a few seconds to return with a tray of freshly baked biscuits and a big smirk on his face. "Melba will have to wait for her elevenses."

"Often travelled coordinates?" enquired Jung. "You can be quick or hungry," laughed Jester.

They all agreed the SAC chef made excellent biscuits, as Mel gave way to temptation and Miaow wondered who or possibly what was Melba. Over the tea break, Mel mooted the proposition of a mini-gestalt to speed up their deliberations. Miaow refused the offer on the grounds that they might find something about the mysterious Millicent or the femme fatale, Fahmita 'Mita' Loor (a.k.a Fahta) the wriggly Stannish double agent. Mel doubted the latter, as Thyme's stories of the times she kissed and hugged him were the stuff of legends but he conceded the principle of privacy.

"To recap the situation, Miaow you won't agree to join our covenant and Dragon won't give you visiting rights to the planet, in case you upset the time lines," announced Judge in what sounded like his sentencing voice.

Miaow and Dragon looked at him as if his wits had joined the bats in his belfry. Judge gave the pair a querulous look and lounged back in his chair.

"Miaow wants to visit Twit or Warden. Warden is on Blaids Watch so he's out unless Miaow joins the Watchers, which he categorically refuses to do. Miaow is a Twit-stringer but Twit doesn't know it and that goes no further than here," explained Dragon very, very carefully.

Miaow nodded and managed to stare at all the assembled Skuide simultaneously. The group became pensive for a while and Mel had another biscuit.

Jung cleared his throat but it was Jester who spoke, "Dragon, SAC is outside of Dukiesland and I'm willing to vouch for Miaow if he comes with me." And to Miaow, "You never know who you might bump into at my office or where we might be asked to go to by a prospective customer."

Everyone knew it was a ploy to get Miaow planet side but it kept within the so called boundaries of the covenant and the Stasis Watch was not blasting out alarm calls upon the suggestion. To Dragon, it got the fiery Miaow off his back and to Miaow, it at least got him halfway to where he wanted to be without upsetting a lot of Skuide. They all put their hands into the middle of the table as a sign of agreement. The Stasis Watch's wail made them all jump back and retract their hands before they declared acceptance.

Their befuddled looks slowly changed as the message behind the alarm came through, 'IT has reported that the Traceries are empty and have a 'Busy, Call Back Later' sign up. IT thinks some big project is taking up all their resources. Such a project is not known to us.'

They gave a collective sigh of relief and Judge adjourned the group as he headed off to investigate what had happened to the Traceries, when the Stasis Watch sent out another alarm which stopped him in his tracks.

"We haven't accepted the pact," said Miaow pointedly, hoping that was the cause of the second alarm.

Hope ducked for cover as the real reason came through. Fahmita Loor had applied to enter Dukiesland, ostensibly on her way to Hoggeralia. Miaow chuckled. He liked the screeching, double crossing little brat.

"I hope she remembers to talk through her hand," shouted Mel with his fingers firmly wedged in his ears. "Maybe she's coming back about unfinished business with Thyme."

Judge did not laugh at the quip. Instead, he groaned, "Not her again. Let's get the pact agreed to and then I have to get tracking the Traceries."

The lack of an alarm heralded the acceptance of the pact.

~~

A great hand held up a ball and passed the other hand over it. The ball disappeared but the mind was thinking, 'It can't be them. They are too busy exploring.'

When I Woke Up this Morning…

Writing exercise: "when I woke up this morning…"
Short Story

When I saw Bryan's e-mail, on my phone early this morning, the opening reminded me of the old song, 'When I woke up this morning. You were on my mind.' He wasn't but a cup of tea was. That was unfortunate as the power was down, again. The cause of the the outage, unknown. When do they expect to restore it? In about eight hours. No power, no water, and the kettle is also electric. Options arose in my decaffeinated brain, drive 20km for a cuppa or start the generator. The latter appeared to be the quickest solution. How wrong can you be?

One cannot get out of the house to the generator without waking the dog. Do not even contemplate ignoring a dog going about its daily routine. Paws, bumps, wet noses and woofs are not the best thing for the deprived tea addict. The dog did her outdoor business and then wanted her breakfast. This means entering the room where the cat sleeps. Guess what, she wants out as well. The dog once fed needs to go out for more doggy business as the cat comes in for her breakfast.

Finally, I managed to get to where the key for the generator shed is, only it is not there. Five minutes of searching reveals I had left in my gardening jacket, the generator is housed with the lawn mower. Key in hand and throat crying out for that soothing cuppa I open the shed. I know it's in here somewhere under all this junk, junk being anything that is currently not the focus of my desire. I move all the jumble off the generator which needs a quick dusting to dislodge the resident spiders. Procedurally I have to connect the cable and then start the generator before switching the power source over to the generator, anti-islanding and such like. Procedurally all is in order.

Fate is always tricky, there is no fuel in the generator and I used the last of the fuel in the can yesterday to fill the mower, to cut the grass. Nearest fuel, you guessed it, 20km away.

Helen Downie

As a child, Helen lived within her imagination where bullies were vanquished by courage, genius escapes or wisdom.

After reading 'Jonathon Livingston Seagull' and the 'Third Eye', she was inspired to share her world with an unrequested essay. Handing it back, the teacher said, "You didn't write it...where did you get it from"?

Today, Helens' curiosity and voice is intact and balanced by personal insights having lived nearly 60 years. Helen believes we all have a Jonathan within, ready to stretch out those wings, and her Seagull now sees blue sky for the poetry, essays and memoir on the final stages of this flight path.

Helen lives in Melbourne Victoria with her husband, daughter, a dog and 2 cats who tolerate each other.

Carol 3

Poem

The moon so high tonight
I see it for you, my
Best friend

A spell of blindness
Presented us all
A different challenge, blindness
Your Eyes always still searched for
the unseeable
Seeing, often deceives, it
Never sees the lacking within

Your character
Your feelings,
remained, always, intact, heightened
instead you felt the unseeable

You felt
The warmth of friends
The soul of winter fires
tenderness of family and
 the tone of our voices and
your love of the familiar

Walks in the park
Were a stumblethon
A bumpathon but
With your Titanium patience
You exemplified
Light

You also magnified
Our lacking
Magnified
Your forgiveness and
Magnified the brilliance of
Surrendering to the unknown

Your patience was proof
Attitude is everything

But this night
With he moon so high
You do not sleep
Instead
they weep, broken
Wanting you to
Mend the brokenness

Longing more
Couch and bedtime cuddles
Needing more
Stories and Park Adventures
Stories of new and old fluffy friends
Stories of Sniffing every thing

The moon so high tonight
I see for it you,
I see you in the moon tonight
A net of light glows
On your woollen white coat
A net of light shines
As you lay, waiting
I see you in the moon tonight
Today was your last

It had been 10 years since I had been home

*Writing Exercise: "It had been ten years since I had been home
and didn't know what to expect."*
Short Story/Memoir

It had been 10 years since I had been home, and I didn't know what to expect. In fact no one could possibly know what to expect after turning into that long driveway.

The family farm was a dream come true for my father when he had purchased it in his forties. It was a menagerie of stuff, animals and people that had become a final resting place for the broken or unwanted.

His forty-acre property was his pride. It had solid fences, the best in the district, 6ft high around the perimeter. But the years saw it slowly being taken over by an ever growing number of rusted ploughs and other obsolete farming implements, tractors, steel and wooden gates, poles, tyres and Dads favourite, lots of fencing wire of all descriptions that had been left out to be encased by soil and grass concealing the hidden hazards.

In the beginning, Dad had set out to convert the original Dairy Farm into a hobby farm. Its state of the art milking shed styled in the early 1900's, with practical walk-through bails and leg chains, became a holding pen for calf rearing, drenching and dehorning and perfect spot to sit down with an empty bucket beside Nina or Barbara, our house cows. Our tribe included Sheeba and Pluto our duck hunting dogs, Kitty puss and Mumma puss for the mice, Billy the ram, Mary the lamb, Arnold my pet pig, chickens, sheep, other house cows, ducks, turkeys and a few other landrace pigs, sheep and beef stock.

Dilapidated outbuildings and sheds overflowed with 'goodies' collected over a lifetime from my fathers favourite hardware store, the local rubbish dump. Everyone in that logging community knew if they needed a certain wheel, screw, nut, tool, trolley, a certain anything, Dad would surely have it. "It may take a week or two, but I have one of those", he would say, and Dad would always find one.

I had loved this place but it no longer felt like home, after being betrayed, scapegoated, when everyone let me down, even Dad. That last visit home, I found suspicion, accusations and drama followed me from place to place, even following me back home 3500 kilometres away, like some mangy mutt.

At the end of the driveway, an Albizia Julibrissin with her delicate fernlike leaves was a familiar friend, a gentle welcome, bubbling a reality that had escaped me and my family of origin, a family who was supposed to have everything, anyone would ever want.

I remembered, the pact; Just get through this; smile, escape to the room, headaches, look sad sometimes, sad is appropriate, just follow everyone else, remember you are only here 4 days!

I remembered this tree had shaded me and greeted my wedding guests many years ago. The Juliebrissin is a Chinese Medicine plant used for mainly profound heart-breaking loss, known as a Spirit tonic, it is helpful for trauma, irritability, sleeplessness, sadness and poor memory. It is also known as Chinese Prozac.

So, after 10 years of sleep, brain pain came crashing back up as thoughts of hurt, shame and dread flooded my senses when stepping into a kitchen, the heart of the house. I had managed to forget, forget about everyone, everything, by screaming at the top of my lungs, in my head, until my silent screams drowned out memories, but now in this kitchen, those memories were back in full-force, and I would once again, have to deal with these people, then, once again, have to put my pain back to bed, just like before…after all there was money at stake.

I was calmed by the sweet smell of savoury steaming on the range and food littered the bench tops. Sandwiches draped in gladwrap, foil covered food, a plate of yoyos and a cream sponge with passionfruit drizzled over white icing was cut, ready for the taking, showing a community spirit of love and affection. I first noticed the lino, slightly worn, as if locked by time, nothing had changed since my last departure, even the wallpaper and paint...this was unusual, as mother liked to update.

A round bottom and long dark hair stood at the kitchen sink washing dishes. Turning to greet, this smiling stranger with out-stretched arms leaned in for a hug.

"You must be Marilyn, I've heard all about you, I'm Betty".

Looking at the bags, asking she said, "do you need a hand with those or do you just want to go in and see your father first"?

Shocked and panicked, I thought, oh, FUCK, what is this crazy woman saying?

What kind of shitty joke is this?

Have I come home because they wanted to rekindle our shitty fake, now dead relationships, surely not, even Mother and my Brother wouldn't stoop that low...you see, what pulled me back here was a call saying Dad had been killed.

I could hear a raised deep voice, coming from the lounge room and it wasn't Dad.

Regaining my practiced smile, I look around the room without seeing because I was blinded by shock, my way of holding onto my imaginary world.

"What were you thinking you crazy old bugger?" I heard the deep voice say.

A hum of voices lured me to opening between the lounge room. There, front and centre stood a shiny wooden casket.

Hell NO! I thought, hiding my shock, then concluding...*I cant, not yet anyway.*

Smiling, I say, thanks Betty, I'll take my bag up to the end room, I'm exhausted. Where is Mum?

She's next door.

Can you just let her know I'm here.

Nimbin

This poem was inspired by the words of a shopkeeper in a neighbouring town to Nimbin. The harshness was unexpected, and an utter contrast to my view about human beings and this alternative community. The shop-keepers attitude reflected such a lack of respect, an ignorance and stigma, the barriers anyone wishing to break free will struggle against.

Inspired to study in my forties, after seeing one too many human tragedies, I completed a Diploma of Alcohol and Drugs in 2008 in my late forties. Drug and Alcohol use in our society is complex, I don't have the answers, but it's not the biggest problem we face. Often, misuse and abuse is a result of underlying issues of trauma like family violence and bullying, the status quo and peer pressure, a culture of denial, projection, rationalisation, minimisation, blaming and sometimes underlying, undiagnosed, untreated medical issues.

For some, Drugs and/or alcohol become that battlefield of dependency within the cycle of addiction. For others, it's only an experiment or occasional fun. The tragedy is that we never know who is going to be entrenched in the cycle of addiction with the constant of cravings and seeking to medicate a discomfort.

Today we also know that environment, exposure to screen time, video games can all have a cumulative effects on the individual, increasing their vulnerability to addictions as their neural pathways are changed and rewired. Ninety-per cent of a child's brain is wired by the age of 3, but our brains don't stop growing until we reach the age of 25, the reason teenagers and our babies are need special care and understanding. I am hoping this poem you may be inspire a rethink and do your own research and see blaming and shaming people is never going to bring about change.

NIMBIN

With my history transformed by study
2008 a year to explore and review
Nimbin main street busy but empty
A feeling of isolation and
Human disconnection on public view

Noteworthy was a shopkeeper
His words spewing indifference
In the neighbouring town

"Shit heap
Nimbin is just a shit heap
They have their drugs
At least we know where they are
We just don't give a damn
They can all rot there, for all we care"

Selling home grown or looking to score
Some perch, watching, and waiting
The numb and needy are for sale
A human zoo with the caged in suits
Now uncaged, with wallets full or empty
Buyers cruise in and out of doorways

Bony young men, mattered hair, tanned, shirtless
A woman, big smile, long in the tooth
Her eyes and teeth denied an age
Purple flares and black tassel fringe bag
Defined her power as everything flower

We protect our children with OFF and NO
Too much time with TV and games
Trains the eyes and ears for that dopamine rise
Innocence can easily get lost in bush green
So stay away (move) from this town

Ignored by Social Justice and Services
No need for syringe disposal here

The sweet smelling cones just flutter
Contaminated filth is left to sundry
Forgotten by inconvenience
Regulars and locals are invisible

The seekers of comfort and ease draw nearer
The lure of getting high is not so easy to resist in the springtime
Lost in fate, confusion or feeling low
When you need to just forget, and want to die
 Feel less pain or have a new adventure

I want to scream
Out!
Love is lost in dopamine
I never made the pilgrimage
I might have stayed on until fate found me
In a rainbow coloured, hand carved coffin

I want to scream
Out!
Life is lost in that dopamine fix
Life is a black opal, rare, precious
Stop while you can, don't waste time
Get away from this town, reach for safety
But they'll continue to come
Tourists looking up and down
"Oh, It's fine, it's only token fun"
A cool place to watch and dream
A place to be the underbelly and
score, cheap green

Barefoot children, matted hair, follow a dog in the street
He takes his time, he stops, they all stop
Together, they sit on a step and wait for someone or something

"At least we know where they are, he said
We just don't give a damn
They can all rot there for all we care"

Remembering Pohutakawa Dreamtime

Memoir

After many visits back to my country of birth, and bursting with reverence, I am in awe of the view of Auckland below. Living up to the name Aotearoa, 'long white cloud', distant clouds blush against a deep blue sky. Like a giant WELCOME HOME sky banner, this welcome draws on many feelings, buried deep in my past.

The low cloud cover never failed to part. Revealed, is the narrow irregular land mass framed by ocean or mud flats depending on the tide. A frenetic lattice of bridges connects land to land over the sprawling city. With a graceful lurch to the side, a burst of engine, the shuddering shudder of hydraulics, landing gear is deployed. Ahead lies the target, the runway. Stretching out into Manakau Harbour, this runway looks far too short, so I prepare to die one more time, hoping I am wrong once again...

Relieved and alive, with bags in hand, my family and I all hurried off to meet up with my big brother waiting at Half Moon Bay Marina. This brother and I shared many things including impatience and a need for speed, so his twin-engine trophy, the "largest fastest cruiser around", was a massive improvement on the trailer sailor and tinnies of our yesterdays. The rush and push of the man was a little more obnoxious than I remembered, but out at sea, my own obnoxious habit of complaining was lost in the great emptiness before us. With slaps of sea spray, I knew exactly how Winnie the Pooh felt about his honey pot, because far from land, the warm sea air smelt *just delicious.*

Our destination was one of Auckland's many playgrounds within the Hauraki Gulf. This Garden of Eden was still intact, and the Tree of Life was found within the vegetation and wildlife, rocky shoreline, sea grass, seaweed, mud, sand and ocean surrounding it. Aoteo was close enough to feel like part of Auckland while far away enough to remain pristine. This was to be our Island home and family reunion for the coming weeks, a first Christmas with Mum and Grandmother we would finally enjoy.

Cruising towards Aoteo, with the distant sight of Pohutakawa trees, our spirits were embraced by this familiar summer friend. These iconic New Zealand Christmas Bushes flagged their presence with great clusters of red, hugging the high cliffs, right down to the tideline. Closer, we could see small batches and expansive homes tucked around the jagged terrain, half hidden by dense native bush and Manuka. While unpacking at the pier, stingrays welcomed us by weaving through the wooden pylons.

Once on land, just like in the 1960's, barefoot children and jandled strangers greeted us with eye smiles, a wee nod, and we had our welcome. Our girls found this warmth, both odd and refreshing. Those smiles were touchstones to my birthplace. With this new Winnie the Poo moment, my heart knew that this was where I would rekindle old connections, make new ones, and on that day, my entire family quickly adopted the only island adjective – *awesome*!

Our new home with my brother and his family was run on solar panels, batteries, and a diesel generator. It was perched on a clearing about fifteen meters above high tide at the end of a long steep drive. The centerpiece of this house was the large deck, and the centerpiece of the deck, a Grand Mother Nikau Palm. Under her watch, binoculars were the flaming sword, handy for close-ups of anything interesting happening above or below, like the daily SeaLink Ferry arriving with the shopping.

This 100-year-old Grandmother Palm wore a crown of berries. Feathered guests, flapped in for a rest or feed, including that awesome Kereru, the hen sized wood pigeons or the cheeky Kaka, hen sized parrots. Those noisy flying machines feasted on her sweetness. Grandma's fermented fruit was a special brew. At times, these birds were a little too friendly, showing the same grace of Bushmen after a long hard day, stumbling and weaving in and out of bars on the way home.

Grandmother Palm reminded me of my Nana, whose strength was in her simple, her presence. An excellent home cook, she was a good listener, a safe haven. Nana had a gentle tone, a kind spirit. With her calm, she comforted with respect and consistency. With her I was free of my shadows, and her nourishment, her unconditional, infused in everything she touched. Her sentience spilled into me.

There was a 200-metre cockleshell path from the deck to the bay below. The early morning bay water was never cold and by mid-afternoon, it was bath warm. There, we wandered the awesome waters edge exploring in the presence of countless unfolding moments. I found peace in the thick brown mud at low tide, gathering up the fat cockles for a cook-up. With peace in such abundance, despite emerging family worries, it was impossible to ignore; peace had surrounded us, and we were trapped!

Cockle fritters were a *whanau* [far-now] favorite, my brother's specialty, along with his guitar playing, that uncovered more golden memories of days past pulling me back to the time, playing the drums on stage with him, at the Rangitahi College Social, in the Downie Von Trap Band. Just like in the old days, this holiday haven had everyone pitching in, kiwis are good at holding hands. Meals were more like a community kitchen than mealtime chores, and we were all rewarded with top shelf banter, the catch of the day of snapper or terakihi, sometimes Cray, mussels and thick scallops.

Most nights ended in guitar, a chorus of chook songs, rum and coke, beer and nibbles. It was awesome. On occasion Dom Pérignon announced a joining of families, a special gratitude or congratulations, but those precious bubbles and flavor were lost on me, I rarely drink and bubbles are bubbles to me. There were so many things to celebrate, and some to heal, my mother never made the journey, a family feud was simmering over a couple of back flips, one involving decisions to buy and sell her farm. Nevertheless, we drank, we sang songs, we ate, and sang more, yarning and laughing our way through any sadness and frustration arising from the Nanny who was lost in action.

Evenings glowed with a palate of distant pink and red. With such little light pollution, this islands sky was pristine like a dark sky sanctuary. About an hour after nightfall, a visit to the *fairies*, the glow-worms, in the banks at the top of the driveway was captivating, especially for the children. Who else has *fairies*? Where else? On occasion, while taking in evening views, an eerie glow twinkling in the bay below appeared, and then just as mysteriously, disappeared. Magic seemed everywhere! The island night sky was darker and deeper and the stars were brighter than anywhere else. The Milky Ways' tiny lights formed bigger, denser star clouds, and they seemed to stoop down, real close, greeting our presence with enchantment.

Modern necessities were more expensive on the island, with everything being shipped or planed in. Most locals had a dingy at least, so could live cheaply, self-sufficiency was a choice there with such abundances at hand. Clean fresh water, was a matter of location to a stream, or collecting the rain. With no public transport, islanders without cars would walk, hitch a lift or ask a friend. The narrow winding roads, were also a meeting place to yarn with neighbors or visitors, even during peak holiday time, if a local had something to say or ask, they'd simply stop you. Even in the middle of the road!

Self-sufficiency and independence was balanced by an understanding of their interdependent relationships with each other within this unique environment. We saw how a workload and skills could be bartered, shared or freely given; something often forgotten or lost in a busy of city life. The residents were a special breed. People like Pam, one of the islands potters, a talent with her studio on the Shoal Bay Road, near the wharf. There, she sold pottery for everyday use as well as other creations like the *flying mozzies*; her humorous take of the more famous 'flying ducks'.

Moira, the Currichs's publican from a long-line of good-Irish publicans; adorned the bar walls with photos of her Irish family and her 100 year old Grandmother. The pubs Seafood Chowder was hearty, it was awesome, with whole oysters, scallops and mussels. At Mulberry Cove, Mal, another local talent, specialised in shell jewelry. The awesome mussel earrings and the awesome Paua shell necklace were our trophies, as were Pams flying mozzies. It became no surprise our girls became proud 'tree huggers', both doing their part to spread a different consciousness when they got back to the city.

Gossip and tensions are found everywhere you find people, but with such diversity within the community, tensions were tempered by the many ongoing reflections and the shared desires and needs of the people. Living a day at a time with many free ranging conversations including rats (the island had a resident rat catcher), the politics of Marine Reserves, commercial fishing limits, big fish, and the weather, seemed to keep the inhabitants connected and mindful of what's important. Everyone benefits when we accept we don't have to like everything and everyone, we just have to listen and meet somewhere in the middle. As visitors, the seeding of that potential, a redefinition of progress, and sustainable lifestyle stayed with us.

We felt such love and warmth in so many places. We were spoilt!

Jan Marshall

After 25 years as a Change Manager, Jan joined the WU3A Creative Writing Group in April 2017, and soon after joined the sister class E-Publishing. She had been working on her memoir for some years and successfully published **Romance Scam Survivor: the whole sordid story** in February 2018. From her many press interviews for her award-winning book she has become known as the victim advocate for scam victims. Jan writes her popular blog Romance Scam Survivor, and occasionally does freelance essays on topics of interest such the ones published here.

As a WU3A tutor, Jan has also co-facilitated a Blueprint for Retiring class and is currently sharing her hard-earned knowledge about self-publishing in her class on Building an Author Platform.

Contact Details: jan@janmarshall.com.au

Twitter: @JanCarMar

Web: http://janmarshall.com.au/

The day my mother died

Memoir

The day my mother died was not like the one before. Then, she'd still been talking and sipping liquids throughout the day. Today, she'd done none of those things.

I arrived about 9:30 am and she was restless, trying to turn herself over and scrabbling about. She was not talking to me. Her eyes were mostly shut. She seemed to be focused inside of herself. I tried to give her something to drink, but even with the straw in her mouth and some sucking motion, she was not able to get any liquid successfully.

I was a bit shocked at how much she had changed from the day before and felt I should let my older brother Trevor know. After she was turned by the carers and settled with some more morphine I texted him.

> Mum even more declined
> this morning. Very uncom-
> fortable trying to turn herself
> over. Not speaking, not
> even able to suck when I try
> to give her something to sip.
> She has just had morphine
> and has now been turned
> so has settled a bit, sleep-
> ing

He texted back that he was just going out on a bike ride, and said he would call afterwards. I texted also to my younger brother Darryl. He thanked me for the update, adding

> Sounds like she is near the
> end. It has taken a long
> time.

I responded

> Yes but visibly declining
> each day now. I keep think-
> ing it could be any day now,
> but it keeps going on.

Darryl had lung and brain cancer himself, and whilst he had come to see mum earlier in the week with his partner Kay, I knew he could not do the daily visits that I had been doing. He did want to get the daily updates to at least know what was going on, even if he could not be there.

Trevor called after his ride and we discussed whether he should come down from his home in Gippsland to see Mum. He was coming the following morning anyway, collecting a friend to go on a pre-arranged skiing holiday. I had no idea how close to death mum was but was very concerned about the decline I saw today. I said I would talk to the nurses to see if I could get a better idea of when she was likely to 'go' so he could make a decision about when to come. We weren't a family that makes a fuss about death. Once she was gone she was gone, and she would not care if he went skiing or not, if he was here or not.

I talked to a nurse then texted Trev.

> I talked to one nurse who
> said tomorrow would be OK,
> she's not at the end yet and
> a more senior and experi-
> enced nurse is coming later
> and I can talk to her Xx.

The more senior nurse explained why they did not think it would be today. I let Trev know.

> Spoke to the nurse, she
> said she is uncertain but
> does not think it will be to-
> day. Her breathing is still
> even and her skin showing
> no signs of blotchiness.
> Though she may go in the
> lower energy of overnight,

> she could equally last a few
> more days.... No way of re-
> ally knowing. I think you
> would be ok to come tomor-
> row, but if you would be
> upset if you missed her per-
> haps come. She is not
> responsive though. Xxx

I had done my duty getting the information out to them and hedged my bets. Now it was up to Trev to take responsibility for himself. Though I had asked the question for him, it was good for me to know what to expect as well. That was the hardest part, not knowing. But I relaxed a bit, just sitting with her, thinking it will not be today, and steeling myself for a few more days of seeing Mum in this depleted state.

My memories of the rest of the day are in snippets. I remember being left alone with her by the carers and nurses. No-one came to see how she was unless I asked them to look after her, to turn her, or to give her more medication. No-one asked how she was or if she was getting any liquids in. Maybe that's because it was now the weekend, and it was a different group of people working who were not so aware of her needs, of the decline since the day before. Or maybe they just left the family alone in situations like this come what may...

As I look at the one short video I took of her that day, Mum is gaunt, open-mouthed, eyes closed, and with breath rasping. I took it so I could show my brothers, but never have. I knew, with her mouth open, it would be dry, but when she did wake a little and I tried to give her a drink, even when I told her to suck, hard, she was not able to do this successfully. In hindsight, maybe she should have had her mouth swabbed, or, we should have used a sponge to give her liquid in her mouth, but no-one suggested this, or even came and asked us if she needed anything.

My Aunt Rita, mum's younger sister, came in the afternoon. With her encouragement, we said to Mum "Its OK to go, in your own time". Rita commented later that when I was out of the room she prayed hard that mum would go that night. She just wanted her anguish to be over. We both knew mum wanted that too.

Only when mum's medication was wearing off was there any interaction with her, trying to give her something to drink, though no coherent conversation. She would swing her arms around, uncomfortable, as she tried to turn herself over. At one time she muttered "please, please, please" but what she wanted was unclear. It was heart-wrenching. I would attempt to give her something to drink, but even though she tried to sip through the straw, she got nothing.

In the evening, at about 7 pm, thinking I would go home I let Mum know. She clearly said "No, no, no", so I stayed. I may have watched a bit of TV, but I don't remember.

About 9 pm she was getting restless, and wanting again to go home, I said this to her. This time she pushed me in the chest and away from her with both hands. I took this as a sign it was OK to go. I don't remember if I said anything to her as I left and the carers came in to turn her. I hope I said "I love you". I expected to see her the following day.

I was in bed when I got a call from the night nurse. I am unsure about the time, but it was about 11 pm I think. I hadn't had a call from the nurse before so it was a bit of a surprise. She said she was calling to say that she had put mum on an hourly watch because she was so much deteriorated from the day before. This was normal she said, when people were in the palliative stage of care. She commented that Mum was quite distressed when she arrived, and she had turned her over and settled her with some more medication. I let her know I was only a short distance away and could come in quickly if needed. She did not think there was any urgency, that Mum was not likely to depart soon....

I received the next call at 25 minutes past 12. Mum had passed just 4 minutes ago. The nurse was surprised that she was calling again so soon, she had not expected her to go this quickly. Another nurse was with her when she passed.

Finally, she had found her way into the next world. I was relieved.

I dressed, called my brothers, and went to her side. It was - she was - quiet now, with a white sheet up to her shoulders and a pink flower on her chest. White giving a sense of purity. A towel was rolled up under her chin. No more rasping breath or sense of struggle in her body. Her face relaxed but sunken into her cheeks.

Some of my friends who are sensitive to energy and spirits say they have sensed the departed in the room after death, hovering.... I could not discern this. I was numb, feeling nothing much except relief, just allowing myself to be quiet, just to be with her. Now I could relax, no more waiting and wondering how I would feel when she died.

I sat with her for two hours until the funeral people came. They came quickly because mum had donated her brain to the Victorian Brain Bank, and her body needed to be cooled as soon as possible. I commented to one of the men on their formal blue suits at 2 in the morning. Their preferred clothing was more casual he said, but they had to wear suits whenever on this task for the funeral parlour.

Mum had seen a friend's body draped with a lovely patchwork quilt and carers and residents line up in respect as her friend was taken out and was most impressed with the process. I asked for the quilt to be draped over Mum too, and she was wheeled out with it over her, a very small cavalcade witnessing her leaving at this early hour of the morning. Into the back of the van, then off.

I went home. Tomorrow would be a busy day, the first day of the rest of my life, without my mother.

The medium densitisation of the middle ring suburbs

Narrative essay, originally written in 2015, graphs updated.

Are townhouses the way to go?

As I sit at my computer in my home office each day there is the bang bang bang of building going on in the block next door, and the one after that as well. I'm in the back unit of what is already a three townhouse development, built a little over a year ago with two two-story townhouses at the front, single garages between each unit, and my unit at the back. My unit is single story and has the luxury of going all the way across the block. On the downside though, it is only 1.5 bedrooms. There is a driveway down one side of the block, and courtyards separated by fences the other side. This development was the first in this part of my street. Now there are two more in construction, and one more on a corner after two more unrenovated houses, that was finished and occupied shortly after I moved in.

These blocks were built up as the standard quarter acre block popular 50 or 60 years ago, bought up by working class people from across Europe who came here after the war, possibly by £10 pound immigration. Traditionally, in my suburb, directly north of Melbourne, the largest heritage has been of Macedonian speakers, followed closely by Greeks and Italians.

There is a Greek community centre nearby, that I often see old (from their grey hair and sometimes stoops) European men go into. It is also usual to see groups of older men having coffee together at the local bakery, or chatting together in the streets in languages I cannot understand. It's not unusual to see the men in groups of four. Women will be chatting separately, mostly in twos. I see them at the local pool too, at TRAC in Thomastown, in the hydrotherapy pool, or the spa, seemingly more intent on their conversations (that I cannot understand) than on exercise or relaxation.

No doubt they themselves built their weatherboard, cement board, or brick veneer and tile homes back then, and have since brought up their families in them. The brick ones are mostly of blond brick, with metal curled trimming on their veranda. Their families have grown up, moved on or possibly away, but styles have not. You can see this in photos of properties for sale or rent – old brownish paisley carpets, old style furniture, and maybe even original kitchens and bathrooms.

Though the homes are often past their use-by date, the gardens are not. Front gardens are usually simple and well kept, a border of geraniums and roses around a square of lawn. Its harder to know what is over in the back garden, but the tops of trees reveal the fig trees, apricot trees, olive trees, and even pomegranate trees. I'm sure there are prolific veggie gardens in there too. It's still possible to see the keen ones who have also adapted their front garden for growing food.

The changes in language use across Lalor show the transformations that are taking place here as the generational demographics change. The Italian, Macedonian and Greeks are declining, being replaced by Arab speakers, Vietnamese, and Punjabi or Hindi speaking Indians. Another variety of cosmopolitanism, with restaurants to mark the transition, is developing.

Overall, in Lalor between 2011 and 2016, the number of people who spoke a language other than English at home increased by 13.54%, and the number of people who spoke English only increased by 6.63%. The cultural diversity is increased, by these figures.

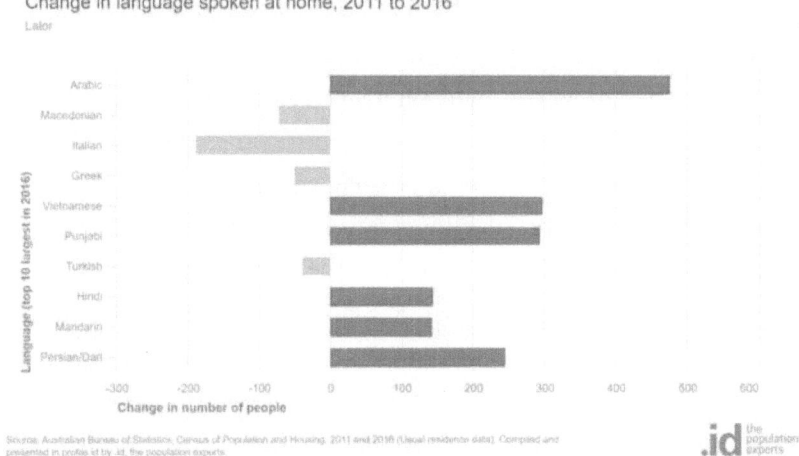

Change in language spoken at home, 2011 to 2016

We know the population is aging, so over the next 10 years, this is likely to bring about quite a modification as a generational change occurs. This is likely to be similar in surrounding suburbs like Reservoir, Thomastown and in between.

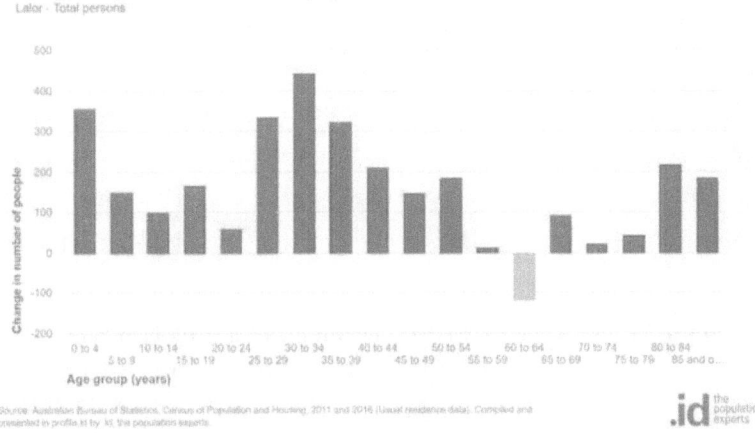

Change in age structure - five year age groups, 2011 to 2016

But back to the building going on next door. With houses built in the 50s and 60s, two types of updates are happening. Firstly, owner-occupiers are building a second residence behind the first battle-axing the block. Selling the second house gives them money to do up their own house. Or they can sell both and move on.

A second scenario is that when old houses come on to the market, the property is snapped up by developers, and three or four townhouses are built on the block, with 1.5, 2 or 3 bedrooms. This is what is happening next to me, apartments are then either for rental or sale. I see this happening frequently on my daily walk up and down the streets as these middle ring suburbs become medium density. This has a number of consequences both positive and negative.

On the plus side, the townhouse with courtyard fits the living standards, no…, 'lifestyle choices' of today, whether it be for the baby boomers downsizing so they don't have to take care of so much house and garden, or for younger couples who want an open-plan style of living. This may also work to keep the young people in the suburbs balancing out the aging demographic, though only until they have children. Then they will mostly move on to 4 bedroom family homes being built cheaply in the new outer suburb estates edged with display homes.

I admit that I like the open plan layout of these new townhouses. I like light streaming in through big double doors from my courtyard, bathrooms next to bedrooms, remote control garages and good heating and cooling. I like the token water tank and the backyard shed also. Mine is designed so the living area goes across the block, meaning it is spacious and light. On many similar developments, you can look down the driveway and see just the garage at the end. I wonder what their layout is like. My neighbour, in the two-story two-bedder at the front of the block, complains that there are no deadlocks on the door and that the kitchen, fitting into a corner, has no preparation space. Perhaps it is a sign of optimal design losing out to the minimizing the cost of building and maximizing profits.

Rental properties like these, because the buildings are new, attract top rental yield, whilst older places are being knocked down instead of renovated. This means there are less lower-priced rentals available. When houses go on the market, as long as the blocks are big enough, the prices are bid up by developers who have done their sums and know that it's a good deal to build 3 or 4 new units rather than renovate one old one. The affordability of an older house for young couples is not there, as they are trumped by the developers. Unless they buy one of the units, which being new, have a premium.

Though I have put some flowers and veggies in my courtyard, I miss the sound of the birds in the trees that used to be in the back garden of the house next door. I especially miss the green of the fig tree which hung over the fence and gave ripe fruit in season. It will be replaced by a brick house wall on my fence line. And fill up my skyline with an adjoining building. If I had moved into my unit with this there I would have accepted it, but living through the change makes a difference.

One thing I notice about all the building going on is that the new houses have uniformly black rooves, black trim around windows, and often the concrete driveways and paths are painted black too. I come from up north where any mechanisms to keep things cool are incorporated into housing and it comes as anathema to me that black is being used so much, especially in parts of buildings and landscaping where temperature and thermal mass matters. I do not understand how this could be considered suitable or sustainable as our planet warms. Summer cooling in these circumstances will chew up more electricity (ie coal) and add to greenhouse gasses.

There also seems to be a problem at the front of blocks. In some I see some landscaping done, and maintained. Others there is no landscaping at all, just piles of builder's gravel left there. The ugliness of this distresses me greatly. And on other townhouses, there has been landscaping done initially, but it has been let go and is now overgrown with weeds. I consciously have to pull back my hands which are twitching to get in and pull them out and have it all neat and tidy again. Please, developers, please finish off with decent landscaping. Renters, please keep it up to date.

If you are thinking you might like to live in one of these townhouses, don't buy a long car. It's a 3 point turn to get into mine, and I have bashed in my garage wall at least once. And out in the road, you will have to get used to giving way to oncoming traffic more frequently as we get more units. These roads were never made for parking on two sides, and two lanes as well, so already its necessary to pull over for oncoming traffic even if there are only cars parked on one side of the road. And whilst you may catch a train into the CBD on trains every 10 minutes in the morning from Lalor or Thomastown stations, if you are driving to the station you will need to be there before about 7:45 to get a carpark.

It is rubbish-night tonight, which brings me to my last bugbear. There is no suitable place to keep rubbish bins out of sight. It is not attractive and inviting to be greeted by rubbish bins as I drive down my driveway, and I see this with many of the new townhouses. Its just not good feng shui! Anyone can tell you that.

Overall I like my back of the block unit, but wonder if in another 50 or 60 years they will be pulling down these townhouses, perhaps replacing them with hi-rise blocks. Perhaps it will have come full circle, and we don't use cars anymore, or maybe we have flying vehicles which land on the roof. Then there will be plenty of room on the roads. I do wonder what the future will bring, and what positive and negative changes moving to medium density will bring.

✦★✶❦♌★★✦

Alone

Three sections of a book, with a working title 'Alone', in the
process of being developed into a trilogy. Early unedited draft
shared in the creative writing group.
Novel Extract

ANYA

Alone. All alone.

Not lonely, or so I tried to convince myself.

Where was my fairy godmother? Why had she not come along and magicked up handsome prince for me? Someone to love me and complete me. There must be something wrong with me for this not to happen, I mused. I was a princess after all. It was expected of me, to meet and marry a prince.

But stuck in the castle, I didn't meet any princes.

Since my father's death when I was just six years old my mother had been so busy with her Queenly duties that she had lost sight of me. She was always surrounded by her courtiers, who were eager supplicants for her attention and favours. In her absence I had grown up with the freedom to do as I wished, follow my own inclinations. I had found I could wrap the nurses and guards around my little finger. And no one would say no to whatever I wished. I had the run of the Keep, including the library, and from an early age had devoured one book after another. And if books in the library did not cover something I wanted to know, I just asked the old librarian and he would go and get the best there was on the topic for me. I knew more about our realm's history, its wars with neighbouring kingdoms, and all the plants and animals it contained than anyone.

As I went towards the stable to go out for my daily ride, I saw Thomas coming out of them. I slowed my step hoping he would go on about his business. Unfortunately, he spied me.

"Lady Anya", he called out to me. "I've saddled Buttons for you. Don't go down by the river path today. There have been bandits seen down that way."

His tone irked me. He had no right to tell me what to do. He was just a stable boy, and about my own age. I would go by the river path just to prove that I could take care of myself. Though we had grown up and played together as children recently I had noticed a proprietary air in his manner towards me, and I did not like it. It was not his role to be concerned for my safety. I knew how to protect myself.

I had started training with the soldiers when I was quite little, trying to copy their movements from the sidelines, like a child's dance. The Master at Arms could see that my nurse was not really interested in me. He had taken pity on me and had fashioned a small wooden sword for me to play with. I kept coming back and over the years as he began to seriously train me in sword skills, the cross bow, and hand to hand combat. I came to love training with the guards every day and pushing myself till I could at least match them in a fight and I was breathing heavily. I knew I was good, though I had never been tested in a real fight or battle. I hoped one day I could defend my realm in battle. However I dreaded the thought that my mother would somehow find out what I was doing before then and make me stop because it was not what princesses were expected to do. The Master at Arms knew enough not to say anything to my mother, or other courtiers, and to keep me as much out of sight as possible whilst I trained with the men. I knew that secretly he was proud of me, of my determination to learn and the skills I had developed, as if I might have been his own daughter.

We have not had problems with bandits this close to the Keep, I thought to myself. I'll be OK. I'll take my crossbow. I was a good shot, and regularly brought back a rabbit or two to the cook. The cook knew that rabbit pie was one of my favourite dishes, and added juicy carrots, swedes and herbs to the pie as well. My mouth watered as I thought about it. I determined that today would be one of those days I brought rabbits back. I knew of a small ridge around which the river curled that was full of rabbit burrows. That would be perfect, I thought as I planned my ride in my mind. I begrudgingly called "Thank you" to Thomas, and sauntered on to the stable with my head high, as if I was a princess without a care in the world.

Just before I turned into the stable, I turned towards Thomas to see if he was watching me. He was, with his hand on his hips. As I moved out of his sight I stuck my tongue out towards him. It made me feel better, even if he did not see it. As I turned back, the Stable Master was glancing my way and raised his eyebrows at me, though he did not say anything. He just continued on working on a broken bridle he was fixing. I knew he had seen the growing tension between myself and Thomas recently, but he had not commented on it, to me anyway. I flicked my black plait over my shoulder, collected my cross-bow from the armoury and strode towards my horse with a confidence that was mostly bluster.

It was mid-morning as I set off, heading north to the tree line, but once past that I headed east towards the river.

CONLAN

I wasn't happy about where we had made camp. It was too open for my liking, but with Donegal in charge what could I do.

The mage, like all mages, thought he was invincible. His arrogance vexed me. He knew we needed to keep our cover and not let anyone know we had come across the border from Welesdeen into Mystaland but he did not take the need for secrecy seriously. The others had gathered wood and made a fire at his direction, and were grilling a skinned rabbit on a stick over it. We were between a small ridge and the river. There were few trees around, and the smoke could be easily seen by anyone nearby, if they cared to look.

Donegal sat away from the fire on a log, with his hood up and face hidden. He was sitting as if in meditation. I had seen him do this before and knew it was his way of avoiding conversation with those who he deigned were not worth his time. And that included me.

Though King Tarneet knew I would dislike the task, he had sent me out with Donegal to make sure he was protected. We were to bring back what information we could about the Queen and her daughter. The King wanted to build a strategic alliance between the two kingdoms, to thus strengthen his own hand in the Hold of Five. He wanted to create any advantage he could to further his negotiations with the Queen, especially if it meant being able to pressure her rather than allow any choice. King Tarneet was ruthless in pursuing his own agenda. I knew that about my father.

And I was his lackey, I thought derisively.

I noticed the horses tied between the trees getting restless with heads up and ears forward instead of their usual grazing. At the same time, I heard the thwack of a cross-bow loosening and dirt being thrown presumably from the quarrel hitting the ground. I ducked automatically, before recognising that the sounds were not close, and were coming from the other side of the ridge. I kicked sand over the fire to put it out, motioning the guards for silence. I grabbed up my own cross-bow and crouching low ran towards the ridge. As I threw myself down below the crest, and shimmied up, the mage landed at my side and we both cautiously peeked over.

On the other side of the ridge, three lengths away, we could see a young woman crouching down collecting a rabbit driven through with a crossbow shaft. I could tell it was a woman because even though her hair fell in a plait down her back, the riding habit emphasised nicely rounded hips, and her jacket moulded her body and showed her upper curves in the right places. She was too far away to make out her face clearly. A horse behind her shoulder trailed its bridle as it took a moment to nibble at the grass. Our horses had likely sensed this one nearby.

Donegal and I scurried back down the slope till we could stand. "I'll take her" he whispered. "She will give us some information about the Queen and her daughter. Be ready to collect her". I nodded agreement. Perhaps this huntswoman was just what we had come for.

Donegal stood up straighter, closed his eyes and gathered his magick to him. I stepped back and watched as the air close to his body seemed to swirl around him, turning opaque, blue then green, then cleared again. He then shuffled up the side of the ridge until he could see over the crest, but still able to stand straight up. Both arms came up to shoulder level, palms flat and pointing over the top of the ridge to where we had seen the young woman.

I shimmied up the side of the ridge on my stomach again and peered over just as a blue thread leapt out of Donegal's hands, sped towards the woman and within a blink had wrapped around her and lifted her up so she was fully trussed and hovering about a foot off the ground. Her horse startled, rearing slightly, swung around away from us and galloped off. "Go" said Donegal. I jumped up and over, and sped towards her.

ANYA

Anya gently pulled her quarrel through the neck of the fat rabbit. It was the second she had caught and she was pleased with herself for not damaging the good eating meat. As she reached for the rope at her belt to tie it to her saddle, she suddenly felt the tingle of magick. As she stood to see where it was coming from, she saw the blue thread coming at her like a bullet, but could do no more than take a breath in surprise before she found herself trussed around, unable to move, unable to make a sound, and hovering above the ground. She tried desperately to throw it off to get free, but could not move her arms from her sides, and felt stiff like a log.

She was surprised, because magick was outlawed in Mystaland, and mages were usually stopped at the border and refused entry. She knew enough about magick to know that she had been caught with it, as she had felt that tingling before. She knew, that because of her lineage, she had some magick in her, though she had not been trained how to use it. Over the years she had looked in the library for books on magick to find out what she could, but they had been taken out when magick was outlawed by her father after a very bad harvest that he blamed on the mages. That is, all except the mysterious tome she had found hidden behind some very old and boring farming almanacs that were from years past and no longer useful. She had squirrelled the book away up to the tower that was her favourite reading nook and hiding place for all her secret keepsakes. There she began to experiment with the spells the book described. She thought it was safe until she managed to create fire, and some old curtains had caught alight. If she had not been as quick as she had been in putting the fire out the whole keep could have been burnt down. She managed to keep the burns to her hands a secret, but she did not go back to her book again, leaving it to gather dust like the rest of her childhood treasures. "It was safer for everyone that way", she decided.

Now, hanging there in the air above the dead rabbit, she looked around, as far as she could see. She had heard her horse gallop off. As she saw a man running towards her she sent a quick prayer to the Goddess Innanae for vengeance against those who had dared to take hold of her against her will.

He stopped a foot away, gazing up at her. He was tall, and though he had to look up to see her face, she knew it would be reversed if she were on the ground. He was broad shouldered, with the most striking blue eyes, and blond hair that fell forward over his brow and fell loose to his shoulders. He had high cheekbones, a square jaw and a nose that looked like it had taken some hits in its time. His dress was like any farmer, except for the sword at his side.

She could do nothing but look at him with eyes wide. She wondered if he could see the anger that was growing inside of her at her peremptory capture or the curling of fear she felt in in her stomach as he peered at her. He looked her up and down, and she squirmed inside as his gaze again met her eyes and seemed to see deep into her. The edge of his mouth raised slightly in acknowledgement of her. She determined she would not show her fear, and made an effort to put on a haughty face, though she was not sure her muscles were responding.

He picked up the rabbit tucking it into his belt, collected her cross bow and quarrel from the ground. He stepped closer and carefully pulled her down over his shoulder, still trussed in the blue magick so she could not move, with her head hanging down his back and her plait just about trailing on the ground. He kept her there with one arm curled around the back of her knees, and one hand firmly on her buttock. She felt the warmth of his large hand through her leggings as he swiftly carried her across the clearing and around the end of the ridge by the river's edge to a camp on the other side.

There he gently put her down on the ground. He threw the rabbit to a couple of other men who were already digging for coals in the fire to get it going again and threw the cross bow to the side, well out of her reach.

The mage was standing still, hands out flat towards her, but with furrows in his brow now at the effort he was taking to keep her bound. She glared up at him, wishing she could strike him down with magick just using her eyes. The one who had collected her ran his hands slowly over her body, checking for any weapons. He took her knife from her belt and threw it over with the crossbow. Though she could not move them of her own effort due to the magick holding her, he was able to pull her hands together and tie them. She knew from her hand-to-hand combat fighting that if she was to get out of this she would have to act swiftly, so she was waiting. She gave him no reason, apart from the glare in her eyes, to think she would do anything. She was watching the mage out of the corner of her eye, and when he dropped his hands, releasing her with a sigh, she kicked straight up at the man standing above her, reaching his most tender spot with her riding boot. But before she could scurry out from under him he dropped on top of her, with his knees between her legs and his full weight on her, trapping her tied arms between them. His breath came in short gasps as he sought to regain his calm after the pain she had inflicted. Though part of her did not regret it, another part was worried what he would do with her now that he lay on top of her. She was at his mercy. His face was right next to hers and his jaw clenched as he felt the pain. He did not seem angry, or perhaps he was showing his control as his eyes roamed over her face, as if trying to memorise every pore. As his breathing slowed, he made no move to get off her, as if enjoying the closeness of her. She tried to squirm under him, but could do little with his full weight on her. Only she could see the slight lift at the edge of his mouth again and his eyes flashing with a darker blue as he looked at her. She did not know what to make of it. She had never been this close to a man, even when training hand-to-hand with the guards.

"Enough" said the mage. "Tie up her legs as well. We have to question her".

He eased his way backwards off her, this time taking care to hold her arms down, and as he got lower, kept moving his weight down her legs to ensure that she could not kick him again. When he got to her ankles, he held them together in one hand like a vice, and tied them with a rope that one of the others threw to him. Then he lifted her up as if she was weightless and sat her against a log.

Joe Galati

Hello, I am Giuseppe (Joseph). I was born in Acquaro, Southern Italy, 19th May 1941, and was the youngest child of our family of 10. At 15 years of age I migrated to Australia together with my older sister and lived in Johnstone Street, Collingwood. My first job was at Mario's Hotel, in Exhibition Street, City, where I worked in the bar.

Then a silver lining was in store for me; as I had been attending migrant English classes every afternoon at the YWCA, nor far from the hotel. The English teacher there was a retired teacher from the Australian College of Education; and she dedicated herself to improving my English. She eventually retired but made herself available for me to meet and discuss my writing progress.

Now, having received certificate 3 in literacy, I loved writing and my two pieces, *Joe's Life Story* and *The Australian Aboriginal Lifestyle and Culture* with the guidance of Whittlesea U3A Writer's Group and intend to continue into the future.

My Life Story

Memoir

Hello, I am Giuseppe (Joseph). I was born in Acquaro, Southern Italy, 19th May 1941, and was the youngest child of our family of 10.

My mother was puzzled about what name I should be called and, as the day of my birth coincided with the feast day of Saint Giuseppe and its statue was being taken past our home, as was customary. Without a doubt she decided that my name should be Giuseppe after the saint.

As a child I went to Primary school until Grade 5. Then I worked for a short time with a blacksmith, as there were not many other choices for me.

At 15 years of age I migrated to Australia together with my older sister Rosina, my senior by four years. Our older brother Pasquale was already in Australia 3 years earlier and was living with our now deceased cousins Bruno and Pina, with their 2 children Tony and Anna Maria, in Johnston Street, Collingwood. On our arrival to Australia, my sister and I went to live with them.

Our cousins did not accept any payment from us until we both found work; then, we were charged one pound per week rent.

At first, I was feeling strange living in Australia without any knowledge of English or anything else about Australia. All I remember of those early days was that the Olympic Games were being held in Australia that year.

My first job in Australia was working for 3 weeks in a Heater factory. Then, my cousin Bruno found a job for me at Mario's Hotel, in Exhibition Street, City. Mario's was near the hotel where he was working as a waiter.

At Mario's I was put in 'The Cupboard', it was a small bar just outside the dining room, where the waitresses came to get drinks to serve to the customers in the dining room. The barman was Italian, and he could teach me to mix the drinks.

For the first few weeks I turned up for work 7 days a week, because I wasn't told I could have a day off. Then, the manager told me I can have a day off per week and, asked me which day I preferred. I said I preferred Sunday. The manager was surprised and said, on Sundays the hotel is open only for dinner and all staff starts work at 5 P.M.

I confirmed my choice to have Sunday off because only on Sundays I could be with my family at home.

So, I began working normal hours having every Sunday off.

I was keen on the job mixing drinks for the waiters and also was, occasionally, reading the drinks menu and taking notice of the prices in general. Eventually, I knew by heart all prices and, the new waitresses were always asking me how much their drinks were.

Having acquired this valuable knowledge and, also being always punctual for work, the manager trusted me to get me trained to do the barman's job on his day off. This included mixing the drinks and cashing the money as well. So, my work increased, but my wages remained the same and very poor at that.

My cousin advised me to try to get a job in the dining room, where I could get some tips from the customers. So, I ventured to ask the manager if I could be trained to serve in the dining room. He was reluctant to say yes; but, on my insistence he agreed.

I started being trained to serve drinks in the dining room, and this was really not my cup of tea. I was feeling frustrated all along.

A silver lining was in store for me; as I had been attending migrant English classes every afternoon at the YWCA, not far from the hotel. The English teacher there was a retired teacher from the Australian College of Education; and she was a very good teacher indeed.

Eventually, I told her that I was having difficulty serving customers in the dining room. The teacher asked me what I would like to do for a living. I told her I liked office work.

The teacher started looking in newspapers for jobs available and found an Advertisement: 'Clerical assistants wanted to be trained at the Taxation Office'. I liked that idea and, the teacher, on my behalf, sent in an application together with her reference.

I had to pass a simple test: to correct a list of misspelled words, and to do basic arithmetic, which I completed successfully.

I started working in the Taxation Office in the Letter section as a Searcher Clerical Assistant Grade 1. My daily work was to receive a number of letters and to go searching all over the floors of the office to look for the files and to attach the relevant letters to the files.

I found this job tedious from the word go, for various reasons: my English was poor and I found it hard to work with the people of a different culture and, on top of that, I didn't socialise well with the people on our tea and lunch breaks. I was continually feeling like I was a fish out of water.

My English teacher eventually retired but made herself available for me to meet her at some places where she was, if I wanted to see her. On one occasion I told her that I wasn't finding my work interesting. Her answer to that was, hard work is never interesting.

I persevered with the job, as I had no other way of earning my living. Over the years I was promoted to grades 2 and 3. This was no relief, as then, I had to find files that other less qualified searchers hadn't been able to find. This was even more frustrating for me.

I knew that I had come to a dead end with my career at the Taxation Office and that I should start looking for some easier work to do.

My best inheritance from Taxation Office was: I had met Jennifer, my wife there, and took her with me when I left.

Jennifer and I became engaged in 1964 and were married in 1965. We had 4 children and began a new family life together.

In those days the State Bank was offering a Bonus of $500 dollars to first home buyers. I already had a saving account with the state Bank; so, my wife and I applied to the bank for a loan to buy a house and received both, the loan to buy a house and the bonus of $500 dollars. My wife Jennifer and I both worked hard for some years to raise the family and at the same time pay the mortgage to the bank.

I was lucky to find work because, in those days, unskilled jobs were available. So, I started one job, then another, and then another. I was still feeling unhappy in any job; the main reason was, I couldn't socialise well with the workmates.

At last, I went to register with the Employment Office as unemployed.

I had been a church goer all my life and attending regularly church meetings. At one meeting in the house of a parishioner, I prayed to God that I would find a suitable job and, the owner of the house also prayed that I could find suitable employment. Well, my lucky day came when I received a letter from the Employment Office, asking me to go to Cushen Clothing Thomastown and apply for the Storeman job they had advertised.

I just did that and, on arriving was told to sit in the waiting room. There was only one other man sitting there.

Soon, a man strutted in and said who wants me? I timidly put my hand up. He told me to follow him and took me to his office. He asked me what I was looking for, and I told him I was applying for the storeman job they had advertised. He said to me, you start tomorrow.

I told him that I needed to give notice where I was working; and, he replied, you can start next week.

Cushen Clothing was producing and selling work clothes. At a later date, the YAKKA Company took over, without any changes being made to the workers.

I started working there as a storemen. The work was heavy. There were two of us in the store, receiving regular truckloads of cloth. We had to unload the truck using a fork lift, and then stack the boxes on pallets and store them away against the wall.

I persevered with the work and, slowly, got used to it. I knew that if I turned up for work, I got paid and was able to pay my bills.

When I heard a rumour that the Thomastown branch was going to close down, I just felt emptiness within me thinking, how am I going to fill in the days at home?

I spoke to my parish priest about it and told him of my concern, and he replied, retire? Nobody retires, just one door closes, and another door opens. This put me at ease.

Well, it just happened to me that way. I was just two years from retiring age when I was retrenched.

I went to NMIT Epping branch to ask what was available and spoke to an English teacher who was running a Literacy Course for grownups who had missed their schooling. The Course was being subsidised by the Government.

I was told that, if I wanted to enrol was welcome to do so, because they needed more students. I felt lucky again and wasted no time to enrol and to start attending classes.

Two years later, when I reached retiring age, I continued the course until I received Certificate 3 in literacy, which was as far as that course went.

Now, having received certificate 3 in literacy, I felt proud and on top of the world. When drove the car, I could read the signs and was happy to look around and enjoy the scenery.

The Australian Aboriginal Lifestyle and Culture

Narrative Essay

Introduction

The Aboriginals are the original inhabitants of Australia, and are also called Indigenous people. They are believed to have migrated from Asia at least 40,000 years ago. They were nomadic and moved from area to area. They adapted their lifestyle to the local climate and natural conditions to obtain from the land all their basic needs: food, shelter, and clothing. They were self-sufficient in the tools and weapons they used and the food they ate.

The Aboriginals were religious people and prayed for protection of their country and their spirit ancestors. They entertained their guests with dances and music, and performing the corroboree when important members of their clans met, and they often intermarried. Different clans perform different types of corroboree.

The Aboriginal's Lifestyle

The Aboriginals lived a nomadic lifestyle; moved from area to area, and built huts called Mia-Mia at each place they settled. Their main occupation was farming and hunting. They gathered off the land all they needed to live, and were self-sufficient in the tools and weapons they used and the food they ate. They lived within clearly defined traditional boundaries in groups of up to 500 people, where they hunted and gathered. They lived in harmony with the land and were safe in their local areas.

The mistrust of non-Indigenous folks towards their rituals and culture forced some members of their clans to go on periodical holidays to fulfill their religious obligations in secret.

The Aboriginals shared a common language and their common connection was to their land and their history. They were connected to larger groups who shared a common culture; and, although their dialects may have been slightly different, they belonged to a similar culture group.

The Aboriginals' Culture

The Aboriginal Culture of Australia is estimated to date back 40-60000 years; and is held among the oldest surviving cultures of the world. They spoke in hundreds of different languages, excluding dialects; and, although possessed distinctive cultural traits, they shared common values and partook in a common heritage. Their culture places high value on ceremonies and rituals. Art and music formed part of their culture. They entertained guests with dances and music and performed the corroboree when important member of their tribe met; and they frequently intermarried.

The Aboriginals practiced Firestick farming, which involved changing the eco-habitat of the environment by burning out specific plants and vegetation. This helped them in their hunting and gaming.

The Aboriginals held objects of religion and of spiritual significance, known as the Tjurunga or Churinga, very dear. They practiced specific rituals and ceremonies to pass on the possession of stone, wooden or bone objects, knowledge of Ceremonies and chants, or other musical instruments. They decorated sacred sites with emblems of spiritual significance and, chants and instrumental renditions such as didgeridoo notes lent support to these rituals.

Current day records show that about 72% of Aboriginals have embraced Christianity, and about 16% do not follow any organized religion. Myths and folklores of the Aboriginals; however, explain the metaphysics of these tribes using Dreamtime. This explains the origin of the world, the spiritual implications of life and death, and the influence of spirits and ancestors on the living; and the loving specific rituals and ceremonies are practiced to pass on the possession of these important objects such as stone, bone or stone objects, ceremonies and chant. These musical chants and instrumental renditions lent support to these ceremonies.

Sacred sites were decorated with emblems of spiritual significance and religious motifs. Musical chants and instrumental renditions, such as didgeridoo notes lent support to these rituals.

Specific rituals and ceremonies were practiced to pass on the possession of important objects, such as stone, wood, or bone objects, knowledge of ceremonies and chants, or other musical instruments. They decorated sacred sites with emblems of significance and religious motifs. Their religion is The Dreamtime.

Dreamtime explains the origin of the world, the spiritual implications of life and death and the influence of spirits and ancestors on the living. The ceremonies and rituals of the Aboriginals are based on the principle of parallel existence of past, present and future worlds.

The Aboriginals had a two-way relationship with the land; they were the custodians of their country and prayed for protection of their country and their spirit ancestors. They placed high value on ceremonies and rituals; and held some places sacred, having spiritual significances. They entertained their guests with dances and music, and performed the corroboree when important members of their clans met; and they frequently intermarried. Different types of corroboree were performed by different clans.

Firestick farming was generally practiced; which, involved changing the eco- habitat environment by burning out specific plants and vegetation; this helped them in hunting and gaming. Farming and gaming were the main occupations on Aboriginal Australian.

The Aboriginals entertained their visitors with music and dances; and performed the corroboree when important members of their tribe came to visit them; and they frequently intermarried. Different clans performed different types of corroboree.

The Aboriginals were safe in their local areas. They lived a secure social structure based on groups that formed of up to 500 people. They shared a common language and their common connection was to their land and their history. These clans were connected to larger groups who shared a common culture; and, although their dialects may have been slightly different, they belonged to a similar culture group.

However, they were not friendly with other indigenous outside their usual route. These people belonged to different cultural language groups, with often very different beliefs and ideas. Strangers were feared as enemies and were often believed to be dangerous sorcerers. Fights and large-scale wars often erupted between these groups.

Conclusion

As we have seen, the Australia Aboriginals or Indigenous peoples were the original inhabitants of Australia that migrated from. They lived in harmony with the land and were protective of their country and prayed for protection of their country and their spirit ancestors. They lived together in friendly groups and were safe in their local areas. They were unfriendly with other groups outside their usual routes, and believed them to be dangerous; and often engaged in cruel fights with these groups.

Lorraine Holland

The very richness of my life is found in my ability to be fun loving and engaging with all kinds of people. This has come from many years of experience raising a family of six precious children in a small-town Romsey, among the gumtrees. I now live in "Nana's House" in the lovely leafy suburb of South Morang where my eight fantastic grandchildren drop in anytime. I have been a resident in the shire of Whittlesea for 20 years and love going for walks around the many walking paths surrounded by mountains and gum trees. It has been a privilege to be able to travel to other nations as a missionary as it has enhanced my life and made me eternally grateful for my life.

My love of writing has been brought to life through the Whittlesea U3A Creative Writing Group, being able to record for posterity my history in the area and try my handing and expressing myself through the written word.

A glimpse of Whittlesea in the early 1900s

This is a story of recollections, a story of a grand lady of over 100 years living in Preston remembering her youth and the adventure and nostalgia of holidays camping in Whittlesea circa 1900.

My conversations with Lois began when I visited her weekly on a Wednesday. She enquired where I lived, and I informed her that I lived in the shire of Whittlesea. Her face lit up with a smile when I mentioned Whittlesea. This is the beginning of her story.

Look into her eyes... even though Lois has had a long and fulfilling life, a life of lots of joyful stories, times of loss and suffering but plenty of LOVE TO GO AROUND. She still recollects at 100 years her years as a young 8 year old girl, running in the fields with her brothers around Whittlesea. See the twinkle and excitement in her eyes as she tells her stories.

I remember going camping on Mr Brown's farm in Whittlesea, it was a beautiful place with rolling hills and green grass and the Plenty River flowing through it. "Oh... the sweet smell of green grass" how can I ever forget it. My mum and dad, myself and two brothers would go there and camp by the river.

It was common for Lois to ask me when I visit her, "Did you go to Whittlesea shops this week". No matter what my answer was, there was a twinkle of excitement in her eyes which would proceed to her telling me one of her stories.

Mum and Dad, my two brothers and myself would pitch our tent on Mr Brown's farm. So many things to do at the farm, frolicking in the fields, going mushrooming, paddling in the creek and playing with Mr Brown's children Jack and Mary. These children loved us coming for a holiday "We have someone to play with". Our days were filled with running, finding treasures, climbing trees and having so much fun, getting dirty and the day passing from endless minutes to hours in a day.

As I visited Lois on a Wednesday, these stories would take certain creative turns and this day was no exception. I want to talk about my father Peter and his connection to Mr Brown. My father worked in a local grocer in High street Northcote just down from Northcote Town Hall.

My dad would go and feed the horses at the grocer's property, attach them to the cart and deliver groceries to local residents and poultry grain to local chicken farmers in Preston, who made a living selling eggs. Would you believe Preston was a new suburb at this time? He would travel once a month further afield to Whittlesea and supply farmers with grain and feed for their cattle and other farm animals. He met Mr Brown on one of these visits. This began a long and lasting friendship with both families. Mr Brown was a cattle farmer.

After a few times up to the farm delivering feed, Mr Brown invited our family to come and camp by the creek on his property at Whittlesea. There began memorable holidays of frolicking in the meadows of Whittlesea. For many years Dad would do his deliveries with a horse and cart but then progressed to a van. This was a step up because not many families had a motor vehicle but we were able to use the van to go camping in. Our sleeping arrangements were, - Dad and the boys would sleep in the tent near the river and Mum and I would sleep in the back of the van. This car had many uses.

I remember on one of our holidays, as we arrived we would set up camp and pitch the tent, collected wood for the fire, we ran around to check out Mr Brown's farm, and here came Jack and Mary riding their horses across to us. This sunny day Mary was so excited riding her horse she asked me excitedly, " do you want to ride my horse?" She loved riding, but I was too scared and screamed "NO, NO, NO" I was not going to ride the horse even though Mary was so persistent, there was no way I would ride him. My brothers were more adventurous and always were riding horses on the farm. This was a memorable day for me and still so vivid for me.

Lois often would ask me, "did you collect mushrooms this week?" - as she would recollect stories of yesteryear as a little girl. I can still smell the fresh green grass and the huge mushrooms we would find, we would collect them and give them to mum to cook, ohhhh the smell of mushrooms cooking in butter on an open fire, how tantalizing, the best mushrooms in the world from Whittlesea.

Dad would take us across the bridge over the Plenty River with bucket in hand tied with a rope, he would lower it over the side of the bridge and into the river, as he filled the bucket you could see the water was clear and so inviting to drink, we loved drinking this water so pure and fresh, coming from catchments up in the mountains. We considered it the purest in the world.

Lois would often say, "so many stories to tell... so many happy memories of Whittlesea" and then she would start again. I remember a time when my brothers and I often swam in the Plenty River. This particular day we had been for a swim and I saw a long black thing moving in the grass I screamed "SNAKE!" As it slithered into the river. Mr Brown said the snake was harmless and non-poisonous, which was a relief, but to this day I have never been for a swim in that river again.

I remember going to the Whittlesea show, many times we would come up to Mr Brown's property and then go to the Whittlesea show at the showgrounds. It is a time and opportunity for the community to come together and experience the best of country life, the rich farming heritage, it is one of the oldest shows in the district. It is known for the rural family based show with many attractions like wood chopping,

Animal nursery, come and see the cattle, sheep and horses, arts and craft display and local food to eat. What bargains you could find in Whittlesea Lois exclaimed.

"Those years of travelling and camping in Whittlesea are the most memorable and happiest times of my life. I wonder what happened to Jack and Mary…"

The Photo at the beginning of this story is the original and depicts Mr Brown's farm circa 1900s. I was able to hand this back to the Whittlesea Historical society and was informed that the family generations still live on in Whittlesea. This is an appropriate ending to this beautiful and nostalgic story.

Colours

Memoir

I woke one Saturday morning with sun shining through my Bedroom window. This would be an ideal day to go on a" Road Trip". I hopped out of bed excitedly and called out to my kids "Jack and Jill" and said, " it's a beautiful day let's go on a road trip". They jumped out of bed and got dressed, talking about the day ahead. It was a sunny Autumn day, we had a full tank of petrol and we love going on adventures. Mum specialised in these, so we know it would be fun. Driving along we passed farms, with sheep grazing in the lush meadows, we saw orchards with delicious red apples hanging from there branches, we calculated there were hundreds of apples ready to be picked.

We pulled over there was a roadside stall with these nutritious apples ready to be purchased, a goodwill tin was there to put some gold coins in to purchase apples. We ate them as we travelled along the road. We were talking and saying mum " where are we heading on our adventure" mum said, " on our way to "Yarra Valley" there is a lovely Bakery where we can have lunch, and then we can check out the shops for some hidden treasures". Jack yelled out and said, " let's play "Hello Yellow", the idea of the game is to spot a yellow car, there is always hilarious laughter when the first person spots it, at the end of the day the one with most yellow cars will get a special treat like a chocolate bar. This was the best day ever, we love hanging out together, what a blissful day. We went to the "Yarra Valley Bakery" and had our pie and Banana milkshake for lunch and walked and looked at the Local shops, so many had treasures like books to read and Antiques, so many to Peruse and find local crafts and local paintings of the surrounding countryside. One painting that I loved was a "Kookaburra" sitting on a fence with a bright blue sky in the background, I loved this so much I purchased it to take it home and hang on my wall. We travelled home our minds full of happy memories and as we entered our home we gaze at the beautiful sunset and consider the best end to the day.

Mum won the prize for how many yellow cars we saw, of course she would, she is the driver and had first glimpse as the cars approached, she is so quick off the mark...."what a legend" her prize, we had to do the dishes after supper.

We went to bed happy and content...

I awoke in the morning to the sound of rain, drop, drop, dropping on the roof, ooooooh no!!! it was just a dream, I awoke to reality in the aged care facility where I lived, "I would love to escape and go on an adventure"... So be it, what marvellous memories I have when the kids were growing up. What fun we had.

The moral of this story is "Love life. Love your family, have fun, Go on adventures, because the time will come when you can't do that anymore, and all you have is MEMORIES...

Conversations with a poet

Memoir

I remember my schooldays in Brunswick. What happy memories, standing in the schoolyard at assembly Monday morning. It seems only yesterday but was 55years ago, how time flies...Our headmaster in his booming voice would say "Good morning students, stand to attention, please".

Then we would sing "The National Anthem" (God save the Queen) and Recite "My Country". This was our honour to do this every Monday morning all my school life.

I have a fascination about this famous lady, Dorothea Mackeller We have read and recited her poetry for generations and it still stirs admiration in Australians hearts, including mine.

I would love to go back in time and meet with her and in a sense "pick her brain" and question her motivation for writing these poems at such a young age.

So here I am......back in Sydney in 1911.

I am sitting on the veranda of the Mackeller family home, "Dunara" Point Piper Sydney, having a cup of tea with Dorothea. She is telling me a little about her background. Dorothea was born in 1885 and is a 3rd generation Australian. Her 1st publication "My Country" was first published in Australia in 1911, she was 26 yrs old when I visited her. Her motivation and love for Australia came from her travel experience to other countries. While staying in England she was often "Homesick" for Australia, she wanted her Poetry to reflect her deep and true love for her country. Her friends and acquaintances in England would berate her and discredit Australia and refer to England as home, this would stir in her a "Patriotic view of Australia as her homeland.

The original title was "core of my heart" and then changed to "My Country".

When she spoke "the love for her country , flowed out," The natural Australian landscape, it's "Jewel sea"

The contrast "the dry and deadly splendour" the vastness and natural wonders.

Spending the day with Dorothea was enough for me to be so fascinated by her love for Australia and in a sense I believe I have a "little piece of her heart " and love for her country.

Mitchell's Café

Writing exercise: Write using the inspiration of a picture of an old railway station.

I was fascinated to see the old railway station not in use, it still looked so quaint. Longing to drive around the country village of "Mitchell's Town" the rolling hills were inviting and welcoming me there. It was many years ago that I would run around the streets of this town, so many happy memories playing with my friends as a young girl, with not a care in the world... These memories brought me back here many years later. The place had changed in many ways, Bitumen roads, a Bank, Supermarket, Fruit shop and a Butcher. Why is the old Railway station not in use, even the rail had been pulled up.

This station had served the townsfolk and families around the district for many years. This station was still standing strong believing it would be used again. Ohhhh the memories of catching the Train to Adelaide. So many trains coming and going through "Mitchell's Town" station, so much chatter on the train, so much laughter and stories to tell, so many friendships formed, if this station could talk, what stories it would tell...

Standing outside the station "What a grand old Lady" still kept well with a fresh coat of paint, bins standing neatly in a row, chimneys standing tall, wanting to be used again, smoke billowing out the chimney into the sky, this Grand lady Crying out "Can I be used again". This was pulling at my heartstrings, what could I do?

I had an Idea forming like an old train, Wheels turning, like thoughts going round and round in my head, like the wheels of the train pulling out from the station, starting slowly and gaining momentum, we can use you again "Grand old lady", I will get permission to lease you and turn you into a café. I will call you "Mitchell's Café" many locals will come here and have a "Devonshire Tea" and a cuppa. Sitting in front of the open Fire place, with the warmth of the open fire on a cold day.

I needed to put these thoughts into action, starting by getting permission to Lease the Station, after a few weeks of waiting anxiously I was granted permission, I purchased a cottage to buy and moved back to my home town ready to make a difference with this Quaint old station, ready to be used again.

I started to be creative setting about getting furnishings in keeping with the age of the building. A good clean and painting inside with rugs on the beautiful timber floor boards, some lace curtains on the windows, white lace tablecloths and a single rose in a specimen vase with lavender and rosemary in pride of place in the middle of each table, it all looked Nostalgic and grand, all I needed now was a story of the history of this famous Railway station.

I started to research and found out when the first train came to Mitchell's station and a News Paper article when it all began, 14th February 1954 when the station was declared open by the Mayor of Adelaide. It served this community for 50 years and then was closed. But now this beautiful lady is in use again and I can safely say "she is very happy" listening to all the conversations and laughter in this place.

Mitchell's café is still going strong and will be here for many years to come.

✦★★❧❦★★✦

Lyn Brandon

Lyn became interested in writing after going back to school as a mature-age student to complete HSC English and Psychology. English necessitated quite a deal of reading and writing and she realised how much she enjoyed words and the creative process of writing. She then completed a Diploma of Arts in Professional Writing and Editing, achieving some success in short story competitions and publication in both poetry and short story anthologies.

Lyn and her cat Puss lead a quiet life in between taking care of her two grandsons during school holidays and she gains great pleasure and inspiration from attending the U3A writing group.

Memo to charlotte

Short Story

Oh Charlotte, what intricate webs you weave. Perfectly symmetrical, they stretch across little-used pathways, often dripping with raindrops. The trapped prisms gleam in the sunlight.

And yet that aesthetically pleasing web is a death trap; a trap so delicate, but strong enough to house your store, an abattoir for your unsuspecting prey.

I agree Charlotte, that your webs are an engineering masterpiece. To shoot fine silk-like threads out of your bum and travel up, down, up, down, across and back, across and back, then change direction to do the diagonal trek is a tribute to your ability and patience. You produce seemingly mathematically exact spaces and angles, but for what purpose. It seems this creative engineering feat is all to catch dinner. Although an efficacious method from your point of view, I consider it such a lot of work to trap a fly.

I prefer a trip to the supermarket where the protein comes already caught, dead and wrapped neatly in gladwrap on a little tray. Of course, I must pay, and you don't but is the enormous amount of time and effort on your part commensurate with a dinner of one tiny fly? The intricate web weaving must take up many hours of your day. Your only reward is to sit, rest up for a while, then ingest the small morsel, whereas I put in as little effort as possible for a much heartier reward. I sit down to a fine dinner, meat with three veg on the side, as opposed to your fare of a tiny-bodied insect with diaphanous wings on the side.

I notice you rebuild webs with surprising alacrity; webs I brush away with my fingers in an instant. A quick flick with fingers or duster destroys your painstaking work. Your small webs in my house do not concern me too much, I keep you busy reconstructing with my regular web demolition. This is a practice I find necessary to stop visitors pointing and sniggering comments behind my back about my lack of attention to dusting. On the other hand Charlotte, you have scary relatives living in my garage. Huge webs hang from the roof; been there for years. They droop ragged and untidy, the product of your arachnid relatives; the big ones that scurry and hide in dark corners.

Charlotte, I take my hat off to you, but am happy to smash your large garage-dwelling relatives with a well-wielded thong.

✦★★&ꙅ★★✦

Camping with Dad

Writing exercise using the following words: -
delicious, wondrous, mind, peruse, calculating, blue, yellow,
gaze, hilarious
Short Story

'Don't cut its head off,' laughed dad, 'just slice through the skin all the way around. We want to peel the skin down, clean as a whistle. Y'know, like a banana.'

The eel's head was nailed firmly to the tree, squashed flat. I stared at the grey trunk, just managing to keep the squashed head out of focus. I could see it out of the corner of my eye but preferred to focus on the trunk of the huge gum tree. I looked up at the leaves. Still wet from the morning dew, they sparkled in the sun. Birds chirped, cows mooed, blowflies zoomed in.

'What did ya say dad?' I wasn't concentrating on dad's instructions, although the dead eel still awaited my unwilling amateur efforts. No longer smooth and shiny, bloody rivers ran down its body. Frenzied blowflies demanded a taste; their gunmetal iridescence surrounded my head.

'Would you like me to do it?' dad offered, obviously a little miffed by my lack of interest in learning the art of eel skinning. At times like this I was sure dad was slightly disappointed I was not a boy. I didn't **mind** and quickly replied. 'Yes please, I think I'd rather go for a swim.'

I wandered towards our tent to change. The grass was thick although kept short by the black and white cows. They roamed at leisure, continually munching, occasionally lifting their heads to gaze at me with their large, brown eyes. Muted cow-munching was the first sound I heard each morning through the thin canvas walls of the tent, although the early morning peace was soon shattered by laughing kookaburras. The cows kept their wet noses to the ground, paying no attention to the harsh interruption.

Dodging the cow pies, I reached the tent, quickly changed and raced down to the river. The cold, clear water sprayed out in my wake, drops sizzling on the smooth, hot rocks. I sunk to the silent bottom, eyes open, trying to catch a glimpse of the small freshwater yabbies as they burrowed through the mud into their homes.

Floating on my back I looked up at the **blue** sky; monotonous but for the puffy wisps of cloud moving this way and that, continually changing before I could put a name to each shape.

Sufficiently cooled, I emerged from the river, fingers wrinkled, and toes puckered, nails soft and clean. 'Hey dad, have you finished skinning that eel yet?' He had. It was as fresh and clean as I was. Cut into pieces ready to be floured and fried, it lay on a plate carefully covered with a tea towel, the edges tucked well in.

'Those blowies'll get in anywhere,' dad said.

Late afternoons we would often go for a walk along rough country tracks. Small twigs cracked under our feet; we jumped clear, eel-infested streams where ferns glistened from the spray of a nearby waterfall. I loved the bush where the big gum trees grew; where rabbits ran, their long, grey ears flat back on their heads, cotton-ball tails zigzagging and bobbing about at dusk.

I barracked for the rabbits when dad had his gun. He would stand very still **calculating** the distance, aim and fire. I wasn't all that happy about it but ate them anyway when they weren't quick enough. Dad taught me how to skin and gut them; we would have a competition to see who could flick the guts the farthest.

Dad whistled as we walked along. I couldn't do it even though I got my lips to stick out just like his, making lots of little ridges along my top lip. I gave up and **gazed** around the South Gippsland hills. The bright **yellow** wattle had long gone but the cherry plum trees dotted along the bush track were laden with plump, **delicious** fruit.

'Will we get some firewood on the way back dad?' I asked.

'Yeh', he replied, 'we'll need a nice fire to fry that eel.'

I preferred not to think about eating the snakey-looking thing. It reminded me of the snake on the road yesterday. I'd peeked through parted fingers to see dad blow it in two with his shotgun. Each piece of snake flew off in a different direction and landed with several yards of dusty road between them. Dad thought it was **hilarious**.

Back at camp I set the fire just as dad taught me. We would sit close watching the sparks shoot up; the glowing red pin-pricks burning holes in the **wondrous** night sky. I loved to have a fire each night and smell the burning gum leaves. I sat with my head back **perusing** the stars; the milky way was easy to find.

As the fire burnt down, settling into a bed of glowing coals, dad gave it a poke.

'Good cookin' fire,' he announced, 'time to get that eel in the pan.'

'I'm not very hungry tonight dad, maybe I'll just have some noodles.'

New Boots

Poem

He rises from his bed of damp rags
trousers steaming in the same sun
that opens geraniums
clinging to rotting back fences

He lurches on holed boots
along the cobbled lane
with the cold of the night still in it
cigarette butts putty the cracks
ring-pulls wink around gusting newspaper

He clings to a brown paper bag
twisted around the amber neck of oblivion
gums chips and ants from a sodden carton
sips dregs from a dented can of Fosters
left near someone's back gate

Guarding his booty
eyes shift left and right
see a shape sprawled in the lane
he swears, moves closer
a spoon, a syringe
a heap of used matches
lay near a good pair of boots

Wretched fingers tug the laces
ease the boots from cold, still feet
a good enough fit
and after all
the kid wouldn't need them
again

Old Dogs

Short Story

Located at the end of a small branch line the railway station was never very busy; only two trains each day. Deemed unprofitable, the line was discontinued, the tracks pulled up and grass allowed to take over. Tom lives in the abandoned station house. Converted to serve as a dwelling, it was offered to him as an ex-railways employee, for minimal rent.

A tangle of pink geraniums supports the back fence. The rotten palings lean over into the back lane, a rough knife-cut between the country town blocks and the old railway line. Cigarette butts putty the remnants of cracked bluestone; ring pulls from drink cans wink in the scrap of sunlight. Tom blinks as the reflection stabs at his eyes. He keeps one hand flat on the fence and uses the other as a shield.

He whistles up the dog, 'here boy, come on', and works hard with arthritic hands to push open the warped gate. Both his gnarled fingers and the back gate are decayed, aged; both have had little care or maintenance over the years. He makes the effort every day to let the old dog stretch his legs in the back laneway.

The brown mongrel pushes through Tom's legs; he's always first in. He lifts his leg, sprays the cracked plastic flowerpot, scratches the ground once, then drops into the dust like a hessian bag. His dark eyes watch Tom squeeze sideways through the gate and force it shut with his boot.

Tom's navy singlet is loose, ragged around the armpits and his wild grey hair sticks out around the edges and from under the brim of his blue cap. The cuffs of his trousers drag in the dirt. Dust puffs over the dog's wet nose. Tom unbuttons his fly and directs his spray onto the lemon tree flourishing in a small patch of couch up near the back door of the house.

He takes off his cap as he tugs on the wire door. It screeches open and Tom steps inside, careful to avoid the edge of the floorboards, rotten and jagged like the teeth in his mouth. His pupils take time to dilate in the dim kitchen and he leans against the table until his vision clears, as well as the milky cataracts will allow.

Tom puts the kettle on, then sits on the back step with Spud to wait until it boils. He sits, elbows on knees, looking around the small backyard. A light breeze blows red petals to the ground and the side gate clicks backwards and forwards. The latch needs repair like most things around the house. Spud cocks his head to one side, listens. He gets up with a grunt, ambles over to check out the falling geranium petals, then returns to slump on the step. Tom smiles at his old friend, content to just sit and think of days past when Spud was vibrant, chasing and jumping at the falling leaves and petals.

'You've slowed up a bit me ol' mate; we both have.'

The whistling kettle breaks his reverie so, hands on knees, he pushes up to his feet with a low grunt and straightens slowly.

Back in the kitchen he puts a teabag and sugar into a cup. Both were within easy reach. Most things were scattered over the table. Half a loaf of bread, an open jar of jam, plates, cups and an odd assortment of cutlery, all out ready to use. The cupboards weren't needed for everyday use; only used to store bits and pieces that may come in handy someday.

Taking the teabag from the cup Tom slops it onto a saucer stained from repeated use. He doesn't like his tea too strong; gets two cups per teabag. Enjoying his hot cuppa, Tom watches the flies rise from the remnants of his burnt breakfast toast and a half a cup of cold tea. He breaks the toast into Spud's bowl, soaks it with the cold tea and feels his way back outside.

'Here you are ol' fella.' The old dog's waiting; he knows the routine.

They have been together for years, Spud was a gift from Tom's work colleagues when he retired from the railways.

'We rescued him from the pound to keep you company,' they said. 'Not sure how old he is.'

Both are old and arthritic now but suited each other, each understanding the limitations of the other.

Spud laps at the food as Tom lowers himself to sit with the dog today.   Spud looks up as if surprised his master has not retreated as usual into the dark house to sit in the big lounge chair. Now moulded to his shape, he spends a lot of time slouched in the chair remembering and dozing in equal parts with Spud at his feet.

Tom squints in the direction of the sun. It's nearly time. The screeching cockies were wheeling into the bush.

'Let's get this collar off you ol' mate.' He puts it in his pocket and scratches the dogs ear, the one with the tip missing. It was bitten off years ago by a terrier before being rescued from the pound. Tom pulls a creased brochure from his pocket, looks at the pictures of people in brown uniforms cuddling dogs.

The two old friends communicate by a look, the tilt of a head, a facial expression. Taking advantage of today's extra attention, the dog brings a ragged tennis ball and looks up, as if hopeful of a return to the days when they played ball until dark. Tom doesn't throw the ball, just continues to stroke Spud's tattered brown coat.

The dog straightens up, stands rigid. The bitten ear struggles erect. Tom recognises the cue. He pushes his knuckles into the step, levers himself up and makes his way around the side of the house. A van is parking near the front gate. Spud stands at Tom's side, licks his hand.

A brown uniform gets out of the van and walks towards Tom, looks at the dog. Tom nods.

'Can't look after 'im prop'ly no more. He's a good dog.' His vision blurs, opaque eyes even more useless, tears lapping at their red rims. He turns away and shambles around to the back door. The van starts up and he hears a muffled bark as it drives away.

Another, bigger van will arrive tomorrow. He must move out, find his way in more sterile surroundings. His bag is packed; pyjamas, a few clothes, eye drops and a fly-specked photo of Spud. He pulls the collar from his pocket and threads it through his crooked fingers while he lays on the bed to wait out the hours.

He doesn't feel the night chill or hear the van next morning.

The Old Man's Hands

Short Story

Twice each day he stroked her soft, yielding teats. His smooth rhythmic ministrations coaxed her to a wonderful release as her rich, creamy milk squirted with great force into the old galvanised iron bucket.

"This feels fantastic, such a relief," Beatrice thought. "I feel like I'm having a massage at a classy health farm even though this old cow shed is rather dilapidated."

The door hung askew and it shifted back and forth in the summer breeze tracing grooves in the sun-baked earth. The discordant squeak of the rusty hinges was at odds with her contented lowing. Beatrice was at peace. Her golden hide glowed in the setting sun where it penetrated the gaps and old nail holes in the shed walls, but her contentment was rudely interrupted by Clarissa as she bustled into the cow shed.

"Oh Beatrice," she said, a little out of breath. "I'm so glad that's over, Dozer is such a brute. He's been after me all day. I'm quite worn out and he's so heavy."

"Clarissa, I wondered where you were today. Is that the new bull you're talking about?"

"It certainly is. The old man put us in adjoining paddocks this morning so we could get used to each other before the breeding season, but that Dozer didn't want to wait. As soon as the old man turned his back, he started pacing up and down the fence looking for a weak spot to force his way through. Didn't take him long. Those fences are old and rotten. He easily pushed one of the posts over and came charging towards me. I've had such a day of it. He's one weighty bull that Dozer, determined too. The old lady let me out just now so I could come down to be milked."

"Well you can relax now, I've nearly finished," said Beatrice, "you can have your turn soon. It's so calming isn't it; the old man's hands will relax you."

"It will be such a relief after battling that Dozer all day," Clarissa replied. "When my time is right I wouldn't mind doing the breeding thing with him. He's very attractive. You should see his muscles, but I won't be ready for another few weeks yet. Anyway, I'll just have some of that lucerne over there while I'm waiting to be milked."

Turning her head to look at the old man, Beatrice thanked him with a low-pitched moo. She could see his gnarled, arthritic hands, useless for more intricate pursuits, but perfectly suited to stroking her teats. He rested his head on her flank. Ignoring the flies which hovered and stuck to his rheumy eyes, he sighed, sagged to one side and toppled from the stool. He lay there, motionless, sprawled out in the dirt beside the bucket.

"Help, oh help, something bad has happened." Beatrice stepped back and forth, back and forth, lifting her hooves up, down, up, down as if marking time.

"Clarissa, Clarissa, come here. He's fallen off the stool and he's not moving. What will I do?"

Already anxious from her day with the bull, Clarissa was no help at all. She ambled over and crowded in beside Beatrice.

"What's happened, why is the old man on the ground?" She pushed and shoved trying to get in closer.

"Careful," said Beatrice, "don't stand on him. Oh no, now look what you've done. You've pushed his leg forward and his foot has knocked the bucket over."

Warm, foamy milk splashed out and spread around the old man's body, then soaked into the dust.

"Oh my God," Beatrice exclaimed "the old man's kicked the bucket."

The Third Age

Essay

I didn't just wake up one morning, look in the mirror and think 'oh no, I'm old'. I've been noticing the insidious creep for some time and then one day all the evidence came together. Gotcha! The epitome of 'old' is there in full view. The evidence is clear; saggy bits under the sides of each jaw, the beginnings of jowls, are there for all to see.

There aren't any pills for 'old'. The pills handed out willy-nilly by doctors are to correct the failures brought on by 'old', but there is nothing to deal with the plain unsung categorisation of 'old'.

I have now entered, what I consider, the third and final stage of my life. I equate my life stages to a boiled egg. The top has been eaten with relish and enthusiasm, then discarded; the middle section, or main body, so full of goodness and life, is consumed with happiness interspersed with trials and tribulations. Now I am down to the bottom which is still palatable but mixed with the leftover dribbles of all that has gone before.

It seems that now it's all about finding seats, establishing a route without too many stairs or uphill gradients and, most importantly, avoiding mirrors. With the natural teeth gone, a look in the mirror is always a shock. Is that really me? My face has collapsed; my nose is gradually getting closer to my chin. My grandsons laugh at the funny faces I can make.

The ageing layers are creased, folded, programmed in line with experience. The body is shaped and moulded by circumstance and chocolate to fit the person I have become. Now compressed, consumed by life, I tread the ponderous path to the end.

I have been recycled to a new shape; a shape more suited to elastic waistbands rather than the neat fitting, waist-hugging type. My thoughts are washed along with the current of past traditions; past reason and experience is doubted and criticised by younger generations.

I turn the page of the calendar each month wondering where that past month has disappeared to. Is it really December already? What will I get for Christmas? Maybe a new car, a silver one. Yeah, that won't happen unless I buy it myself, but I can dream. I'm getting good at that, day-dreaming, that is. The arena of my mind is a busy place. If only I could remember all the mind-boggling thoughts that pass through it.

The path to the mysteries of the original me leads inwards. By peeling back the layers, like exposing a nest of Russian dolls, the person I was can be found in there somewhere. However, my façade hides my fundamental vibrancy and shows only an eccentric old biddy (battle-axe, hag, sex kitten) who oohs and aahs over roses.

Maralyn Frances

As a little girl, Maralyn was fascinated by word meanings and derivations. Later, after gaining Bachelors and Masters Degrees in English Language, she lived in numerous countries and had a diverse career, including teaching students of all levels, working as a real estate agent, a research assistant for a politician and a librarian. Although she always wanted to write, divorce, single parenting and working full time left little time for creative endeavours so it was only after retirement that she began to write in earnest. So far she has written a number of short stories and completed one novel.

Love in a Time of Old Age I –
Dancing

Memoir (names have been changed)

At the age of sixty-nine I decide that it's time to look for love again. Dance lessons might be the way to go to broaden my social horizons. Unfortunately, at my first class, I begin to realise that dancing ain't what it used to be. You can't just get up and have a friendly waltz or foxtrot with someone. No. It's all progressive sequence dancing now, New Vogue, with countless choreographed steps that give me a headache and quite a few men sore toes. Still, they're gracious in their pain, the men, I mean, not my toes!

The bright spot in the evening is that I win the door prize, a large block of Cadbury's chocolate. Since I don't eat that stuff, I very altruistically break it up and offer it around, thereby acquiring my first suitor in more than twenty years.   Ron is tall, distinguished-looking and a reasonable dancer. We chat, he phones and we meet for coffee the next day in Eltham. We get along like a house on fire, laughing easily, the three of us. Yes, that's right. Dee, his deceased wife is there, keeping a watchful eye on us, and casting my accomplishments and attributes into deep shadow. I soon discover that she's ever-present.

'She was beautiful when I met her at sixteen and she was beautiful when she died,' he tells me.

I nod. Uh-huh. It must be very hard to lose someone when you've been together all those years. And it's only been eighteen months since she died. The man and I have only just met, so I need to let him talk about her. Catharsis. I guess we have to clear this background stuff out of the way first.

The lady was so beautiful that men stared at her. Before she succumbed to breast cancer, Dee looked like Katherine Hepburn apparently, and Ron was honoured that she had loved him. She was really too good for him, he tells me, and he adored her. She was a wonderful cook, an amazing mother and a sex goddess all rolled into one extraordinary woman.

They enjoyed watching porn together and she wanted to try everything. *Oh my!* She was an adventurous sex goddess, it seems. He begins to fill in details. Tongues and other anatomical parts are mentioned.

O-kay! Squirm. I'm fairly broadminded – I believe in the rights of consenting adults and all that, behind closed doors – but this is, perhaps, a tad too much information on a first get-together with a complete stranger. Will it enhance my overall happiness in life to know these intimate details about someone else's sex life? I suspect not.

I shift uncomfortably in my chair and give a metaphorical wave of the hand. *Hello. I'm here! Across the table! Yoo hoo!* He doesn't notice, absorbed as he is in the past.

She died in bed beside him, apparently. *How awful. Poor man.*

'I'm no longer afraid of death,' he tells me, 'because I know she'll be there, waiting for me when I go...'

I try to nod sympathetically.

'...so I'm just filling in time here.'

Great! I'm feeling more and more appreciated by the minute. This is all very sad but what on earth are you doing here with me, Ron, apart from using me as a sounding board? You're stuck. You need therapy or a grief-counselling group.

He tells me about a friend of his, whose wife died four years ago. 'He understands. He feels the same way I do. He's got a girlfriend but he says he'll never get over his wife.'

Lucky girlfriend! I wonder if the poor woman knows she comes a very distant second to a memory? I'm silent, pondering the absurdity of life and my current situation. *Why are you telling me this, Ron, if you hope to have a relationship with me, which, I assume, is why we are sitting here now?*

I simply can't think of anything appropriate to say in response to the man's extraordinary revelations. He shoots me a contrite look. 'I know I'm talking too much about Dee and I shouldn't.' He leans forward with an earnest look, putting his hand over mine on the table. 'But I'll just tell you about the time when she…'

Sigh! Did I remember to take the chicken out of the freezer to defrost for tonight? And I need to buy some coriander at the supermarket on my way home, and some soy milk. I wait until he finishes recounting the amazing exploits of his dear, departed Dee.

I put down my coffee cup. 'Umm, look.' I say. 'I'm a fairly direct person, so I won't beat around the bush. I have every sympathy for you, Ron. I can't imagine what it's like to lose your soul mate after so many years, but I'm not what you need right now. And you are not what I need either. I don't think you're ready to get involved with anyone else, yet. Perhaps it's too soon. Perhaps you'll never be ready. I don't know.' I shrug. 'I'm sorry.' *Why am I apologising?* 'I'm not going to have a relationship (dating code for sex) with you but I'm happy to be your friend. Still, I guess that's not what you're looking for.'

He's surprised at first, and then indignant. He glares at me as if I'm being unreasonable. 'So what do you want?'

'I guess I want someone who feels about me the way you feel about Dee.'

He frowns, clearly affronted, as if I'm sullying something precious, asking for something outrageous and I clearly am in his eyes. 'So you want exclusivity, do you?'

Now it's my turn to pause. I speak slowly. 'I haven't thought about it in those terms but, yes, I guess I do, eventually.' I study him curiously. 'What are you looking for?'

He stares straight into my eyes. 'Friendship with benefits.'

Sex with no commitment and no responsibility, you mean. The stereotypical male fantasy. Good if you can get it, I suppose, if that's your thing. I sigh. When is the man going to grow up? He'd better hurry. Not much time left. He's already seventy and the clock is ticking, as they say.

I look at him. 'Not with me, I'm afraid.' I push back my chair and stand. 'Good luck.' There are, I've heard, websites for people who are into casual relationships. Tinder, for example. I don't say what I'm thinking.

He scowls and can't resist a parting shot. 'If you want to find a man,' he snaps, 'you need to be softer and sweeter.'

Well, isn't that just dandy, unsolicited advice from an offended man.

I pause by his chair and look down at him. 'Uh-huh, and, no doubt, Dee was soft and sweet.' I tip my head and watch his face.

'Yes she was. She was very gentle. Even so, she always got what she wanted in the end. She was the iron fist in the velvet glove. '

And probably very manipulative. I think she knew how to play you like a fiddle, Ron.

'Even so, I always knew where I stood.'

I nod at him. *I know where I stand, too, and it's not beside you, my friend.* I thank him in my softest and sweetest voice, pay for my own coffee as he glares at me, and leave.

Love in a Time of Old Age II – Dancing the Second Time Around

Memoir (names have been changed)

After my first disastrous attempt at dating, my next little foray into the mysterious world of aging, newly single men sees me outside my local pub waiting for Frank. He's a student of the *Charmaine*, the *Tangoette* and the *Barclay Blues,* who has two large, left feet. He's tall, rumpled looking and gangly, with a pair of round glasses and puffs of grey hair on the top of his head and behind each ear. Still, he seems friendly and very keen.

He dogged my footsteps on my second visit to the dancing class as I stumbled through the complexities of the *New Vogue*. He knows the steps but he's a stomper. No rise and fall. He wears slightly grubby, thick-soled, sneakers. Not your usual dancing footwear.

I make a resolution not to pass judgment too hastily, even though, when escorting me to my car after our class, he tries to kiss me on the lips. But I'm still adept at avoiding such encounters – lots of practice in younger days – and I turn my head, so he's forced to kiss my cheek instead. First black mark. Men! Some things never change. Even at an advanced age.

When he proposes that we have a drink together, I hesitate but then I remind myself about my resolution not to be too critical. I suggest that we meet at a wine bar in the city but he objects that he doesn't go into town. It's too hard to park, apparently. Hmm, second black mark. He prefers pubs anyway. 'I'll come to your local,' he says. 'It's not far from my place.

'I don't generally like pubs,' I protest.

He's very insistent. I sigh and give in. Third black mark.

We meet outside the venue. We walk up red-carpeted stairs into a large room. It's a big barn of a place with an expanse of empty tables, deserted except for the barman and a lone waitress folding serviettes on the far side of the room. Near the bar, there's a small lounge area with a dark red, leather lounge, a glass-topped table and a couple of tapestry-covered chairs. I head for the table and chairs.

'I want to sit next to you on the lounge,' he says.

The idea makes me uncomfortable. I still remember his attempt to kiss me when I'd only just learned his name. 'Why? I prefer to face you when I'm talking to you.' I sit at the table and stare at him, silently daring him to object. I suspect he'd prefer beer but he buys two glasses of wine. He carries them over to the table, looking unhappy and sits reluctantly.

'Tell me about yourself,' I say, sipping my wine and studying him across the table.

He seems a bit confused. 'What do you want to know?'

Ho hum. This guy is going to be hard work. 'OK. I'll go first.'

I tell him some details about myself, my family and my situation. 'And you? I assume you're divorced?' Good to get that one cleared up straight away.

'No, not yet.'

Uh-oh! Five black marks and a big, red warning signal in one hit. 'OK. So what's happening?'

'I just moved out.' He fiddles with his drink. 'We weren't getting along. I have my needs and my wife wasn't fulfilling them. I had to turn elsewhere.'

Good grief! I stare at him. *Is this guy for real?* I can't believe what I've just heard. Is that supposed to be a point of attraction? Has he heard of rubber dolls? We've accumulated so many black marks in the space of ten minutes I've lost count. Does this guy have any idea of the impression he's creating? Obviously not. He's looking for sympathy, and a compliant woman. *Bad luck, mate. You've picked the wrong one.*

I hazard a guess. 'So you've been having affairs, have you?' Of course, I tell myself, he could mean he's been buying it.

'Only towards the end,' he says.

Only towards the end! And that makes it OK? So your wife won't come across and that justifies you playing around? Full marks for fidelity! Black marks off the scoreboard and you don't even realise it.

I chew my lip. *Where to go from here? What can I talk about to this blithely unaware man?* Deciding to leave the marital shipwreck alone, I head for safer waters. I pick the most inoffensive of topics. 'OK. So what sort of food do you like, Frank?'

He frowns. It's obviously a difficult question, so I wait. Italian? Greek? Turkish? French? Mexican? Thai? Eskimo?

'I like pizza … and chicken and chips.'

Wow! A sophisticate. How soon can I extract myself from this situation without offending him?

He stands abruptly. 'I want to sit next to you.' He walks over to the lounge, sits, pats the seat beside him and waits expectantly for me to join him. Unless I want to be rude – and I don't –I have no choice but to follow. There is something vulnerable in the man's eager naïveté.

I sit and he moves himself so close to me that his leg is pressing hard against mine. The lounge cushions are soft – probably well used - and he's heavier than I am so I roll against him. Does he intend to climb onto my lap? I try to move away but it's difficult struggling out of the depression our bodies have made in the leather lounge. I look at him. 'You're too close, Frank. You're making me feel uncomfortable. Please can you move back.'

He collapses like a pricked balloon. 'Oh!' he says. He looks like a small boy, about to cry.

'What is it?' I stare at him, bemused.

'That means you don't want to have a relationship with me.'

He's right. I don't, but I can't quite see how he's come to that conclusion, based solely on the fact that I would prefer that he doesn't sit on top of me. I'm mystified. 'How do you figure that out?'

'I needed to sit next to you to find out if you'd let me touch you. We could have stayed all night in those chairs, looking at each other across the table and just talked and I wouldn't have known.'

I gaze at him in astonishment. 'But Frank, isn't that what we're here for, to talk and get to know one another?'

He looks utterly forlorn, downcast. 'There's no point. I know now that you don't want to have a relationship with me because you won't let me touch you.'

My God! This guy's in his late sixties by my estimate. He's been reading too many relationship quizzes in Cosmo. He's likely to move onto shared toothbrushes as a sign of true love soon. If the price of romance is sharing someone's toothbrush, then I'll hie me to a nunnery forthwith. I'm caught between a rock and a hard place. I want to challenge his ridiculous, immature notions. On the other hand, I don't want to encourage him. I frown. What's the point of bothering anyway?

'You're pushing me too fast, Frank. I've been on my own for a long time. I don't even know why we're having this conversation. We hardly know one another.'

He looks glum and shakes his head.

I've had enough. The situation is clearly unsalvageable. I can't wait to get away. I opt for the direct departure: the clean, surgical separation. I finish off my wine and stand. 'I'm sorry but I'm afraid this isn't working between us. All the best and thanks for the wine.' I head for the door, aware that he's staring miserably after me. Oddly enough, I feel sorry for him but not enough to stay and continue the conversation.

Driving home, I take stock. No more dancing for me! I used to love it and I was good at it, but now it's just hard work – headache inducing – and it seems to attract some very strange men. Perhaps I'll have better luck with online dating.

Love in a Time of Old Age III - Online Dating

Memoir (names have been changed)

OK! Online dating! I read an article in *The Age* recently about the growing popularity of online dating for seniors. It features a large photograph of a man I know, a man considerably older than me, clutching a lady of advanced years around the waist. The two of them are smiling like happy Cheshire cats and they claim to be euphoric about having met online. They apparently met in a big, romantic click, in more ways than one.

I give the matter some thought. If they can do it, why can't I? So, after much anxious cheek chewing and frowning and procrastinating, I decide to take the plunge but which site should I choose?

There are numerous ones for those hoping for love (or sex!) to brighten their lives. Some of these organisations have realised that the seniors market is a profitable one and they hold out hope to the Over 40's or 50's or 60's. I'm not sure which of the many sites to give my custom to but I finally screw up my courage, have my photo taken by a friend, write a profile and force myself to click the Send button, twice, on two different sites, RSVP and eHarmony.

I've been a daring dater for three and a half weeks now! Three and a half weeks! I've had a lot of responses already. Very good for my ego after such a long relationship drought! On RSVP, these initial online contacts are called 'kisses' and on eHarmony they're called 'smiles'. I prefer the term 'smiles'. 'Kisses' is too intimate. Still, the designers of the RSVP site failed to consult me when they were choosing their terminology. Remiss of them but there you are!

I've received quite a few 'smiles' and 'kisses' in the last three weeks. I've rejected a few, nicely – the websites have prerecorded messages for that purpose – and been rejected by a couple of men, as well. I was a bit demoralized at first, but you get used to it pretty quickly. I've had coffee with three frogs and two toads but none has turned into my prince as yet.

Perhaps I'm being too impatient, but dating's sure not like it was when I was young. Then I was beating guys off with the proverbial stick. The recent photo I put online is a flattering one but I'm just not everyone's cup of tea – I'm too direct and outspoken for a lot of men – and they aren't my hot brown beverage, either, as I have discovered.

I've read the guidelines on one site for would-be Romeos and Juliettes. 'In your profile, be honest, but don't limit yourself by being too specific. You could deter potential admirers.' I consider this advice. What rubbish! It depends what you want. I've been on my own for a long time and I can see myself continuing on that way if need be. I'm not desperate and I'm not prepared to take on all-comers.

There are some things I'm willing to be flexible about and some that are deal breakers. I'm looking for someone special to add to my quality of life, not detract from it. I want to fall in love again and I'm not prepared to compromise, which may not be the best way to start out. Still, I guess it's worth a try.

My profile is, therefore, contrary to the advice of the website experts, fairly specific. I'm a Buddhist and left wing by inclination. I make a concession by changing 'Buddhist' to 'Spiritual but not religious' but I refuse to change 'left-wing' to 'swinging voter'. If I'm to believe all the male online profiles I've read lately, the country is filled with swingers and fence sitters. Lots of sore backsides! No wonder we're in such dire straits and I don't mean musical ones!

Mr Right doesn't have to share all my beliefs but he does have to be tolerant of them. I'm looking for someone well presented, lively, educated, intelligent and tall. It would be a bonus if he actually showed some interest in me as well, rather than deafening me with fascinating facts about himself. Is that too much to ask? My daughter says I'm being shallow, looking for a tall man but why is it shallow? Isn't it just realistic? We all have preferences after all.

Some women like Asians or Africans or men with blue eyes or blond hair. A friend told me today she isn't interested in men with red hair. Jacqui Lambie, one of our erstwhile politicians, announced on TV – or radio, or both – with breathtaking candour, or, perhaps, a misguided sense of humour, that she wanted 'a rich man with a big package'. *Such eloquence! Such graciousness, Jacqui! Hmm! Perhaps I won't include you on my dinner party guest list, after all. Sorry!*

Some men want a small woman, or a busty blonde or a woman who is 'financially independent', whatever that means. Independent of what? A man I met for coffee asked me how he should go about declaring his earnings to Centrelink for his pension but his profile states that he wants a 'financially independent woman'. I guess he means rich, or a generous soul with more cash than he's got, who's willing to share it with him. Good luck with that one!

Another man, whose profile astonishes me, announces online that he's looking for a self-funded retiree who doesn't have an STI! Really? Does he think that everyone else is happy to be infected by a potential partner? I don't want a man who picks his nose in public either or who has smelly feet or dirty fingernails but something tells me it's better not to include those preferences in my profile.

But I'm getting ahead of myself! As I said, I'm attracted to tall men. I can't help this. I just am, so I live in hope. Sadly, Brad Pitt, George Clooney, Robert Redford, Pierce Brosnan, Paul Newman and Sean Connery all overlooked my charms – well, they do hail from other countries after all, and one is dead, which is a bit of a turnoff. But you never know, do you? Perhaps there's a rich, tall, available man out there with a big package who is just waiting for someone like me. *(Back off, Jacqui!)* I'm prepared to compromise on the looks, but my future partner does have to have a sense of humour and bit of life in him. I'm not impressed by men who are dead from the neck up, or down!

So ... onward to online dating.

As with everything, I discover there are some traps for newbies like me, such as much younger men who, for some mysterious reason, want a woman forty or fifty years their senior. *A Mother Complex? Greeeat!* So far I've had three junior Romeos contact me from Sydney, Adelaide and Tasmania. Sorry guys, no money to speak of! My face is my fortune and it's acquiring more wrinkles every day. Two of my Adonises (Adonii?) have since been removed from the site because of complaints by other women. Oh, so I wasn't the only lucky, mature woman they fancied? *Damn! And it was so good for my ego, too!*

Men who don't want to spend any money are another challenge to be wary of. You pay upfront to join eHarmony so you can email one another to your heart's content, without incurring any extra charges. RSVP, on the other hand, advertises that it's free but, as I soon discovered, this isn't quite true. It doesn't cost to join in the first place and you can make, or reply to, an initial contact with a so-called 'kiss', for free. After that, one party has to pay by using a pre-purchased stamp to continue the conversation.

The expectation is that the initial contactee will pay. When a younger man keeps sending me repeated 'kisses', instead of paying for email contact, I assume he's new and doesn't understand how the system works, so I use one of my stamps to contact him. Silly me! He understands all right. He's one of the men who is later removed from the system, presumably for bombarding older women with 'kisses' in the hope that they'll cough up, as I did. RSVP refunds my stamp, much to my surprise. Nice of them!

Another warning footnote to would-be daters! Beware of the recently widowed, unless they've attended grief counselling or had therapy, or unless considerable water has passed under the relationship bridge since the demise of their beloved spouse. As I know from my previous experience with the devoted and grieving Ron, you can't compete with a dear, departed ghost, especially when she's larger than life and sexier in death than she ever was in the flesh. The pedestal is too high and too unstable. It might just collapse if you try to scale it. And who wants to play second fiddle to an idealized memory anyway?

I meet a man at a coffee shop in Warrandyte. He's balding and wearing elevator shoes. In his profile photo, he looks thoughtful and manly in a black leather jacket and he has an online sense of humour so I make an exception for him. We've barely sat down and ordered our coffee when he starts to talk about himself, his daughter, her boyfriend, his son, his dog, his opinions on education and politics and ... it goes on and on. My goodness! Is he nervous or was he born this way, bursting forth from the womb in full verbal flight? I nod and smile and insert an occasional 'Uh-huh!' whenever he pauses to draw breath. It's not often that someone can talk me under the table but this man manages it. What he lacks in height, he makes up for in garrulousness. I can feel my energy draining away as he talks. Finally, after three quarters of an hour, it's too much for me. I can't stand it any longer. I hold up my hand.

'Derek, stop!'

He looks startled.

'You haven't stopped talking since we sat down and you haven't asked me a single question about myself.'

We part amicably enough – he's a nice man after all, albeit nervous and/or self-absorbed and boring as hell – shaking hands in a civil manner in the carpark behind the café. We agree that perhaps a relationship won't work between us.

My parting from the redneck racist in Doncaster Shopping Town is not so civil, but we won't talk about that! We all make mistakes.

I am developing a promising online relationship with an engineer from out of town. He appears to tick most of my boxes. He's tall and has a degree and we agree on matters political and spiritual. Then, at the end of a long email about his (largely failed) previous relationships with his children and other women, comes an astonishing statement, a real gem: *I would be concerned that being out of an intimate relationship, you would lack some skills. This would be concerning to me because I have talked with and met many women from RSVP and eHarmony and see how lack of skill [sic] gets in the way of good and intimate relating. Maybe we want different things anyway, and that is ok, but it's good to find out early on.*

I'm gobsmacked! Skills! The arrogance of the man! What a surprise that his previous relationships haven't worked out! I'm sure he manages to deduce, from my not-very-tactful reply, that my verbal and writing abilities have not been diminished by celibacy or increasing age! But I'm fairly certain that they aren't the skills he's concerned about! Still, he needn't worry. He'll never get to explore my skills, now, or at any other time, for that matter.

Then, of course, there's the delightful man, an education lecturer, who tells me in all seriousness, that he's worried because I've been celibate for so long. 'Things change,' he confides. I stare at him. What exactly is his concern: physical, psychological or spiritual? Physical! 'It closes up you know,' he confides, 'if you don't use it.' I am flabbergasted. And this from a man with five children! So it seems that I'd better stick my finger up my nose regularly to stop it from closing up!

O-kay! Back to the drawing board, er, website!

It astonishes me that some men publish photos of themselves looking utterly miserable or forbidding. One man posts a photo of a bare brick wall. What message is that supposed to convey, that he's as thick as a brick, or a blank slate, or is he simply technologically incompetent? Others are smiling happily with their arms wrapped around the waist of a woman. What are they looking for? A threesome? Maybe they should join the Casual Liaisons Group. On the other hand, perhaps these men are widowers hoping to demonstrate how loving they were to their former wives or dead spouses. Either way, not appealing!

Then there are the men who call themselves enticing nicknames in their efforts to be different. Wee Willy smiles happily into the camera. No! Really? And you're advertising it? Astonishing, I know, but true! I kid you not! Sorry WW, you're unlikely to win Jacqui Lambie's affections, or mine! And then there's WangKing. You don't need a partner, do you? Perhaps you should change your pseudonym to WangKer. Either way, too much information, thanks.

There are the very ordinary-looking men who tell you how handsome they've been told they are. Excuse me! By whom? Your mother? Your daughter? Blind Freddie or Fredericka!

In addition to fence sitters with sore backsides, the country is filled with boyish, aging men whose friends have reportedly described them as 'looking and behaving younger than I am.' Well, that's what friends are for, to tell you what you want to hear. And why try to persuade me, when I can see from your photo, that you'd make Methuselah look like a teenager? These immature men also describe themselves as intelligent, gentle, romantic, caring, sensual, tactile (code for, I want sex!) SNAGs who love chick flicks (chick flicks!!), rom coms, candle-lit dinners and walking hand-in-hand on moonlit beaches. Considering how wonderful they are, I'm surprised that they're lonely and divorced!

Yesterday I viewed the profile of a man posing in the middle of a row of naked, life-sized, female statues. Romeo is facing the camera while the women are facing away. He's grinning in a lecherous manner while he clutches a bronze butt cheek in each hand. Hmm! No wonder the women have their backs to him.   Another man has a racing bike resting against his thigh somewhere in the Great Outdoors. He's reaching above his head to clutch an oversized pink satin bra that's dangling from the tree above him. Perhaps he should go looking for Dolly Parton with the watermelon-sized breasts instead of posting his profile online! Ride on, my friend. Ride on!

And these are seniors, supposedly, in age, if not maturity! What is it with these guys? Hasn't anybody told them that most women don't appreciate locker room humour, either photographic or written? Perhaps I should set up an online coaching business for men who haven't got a clue how to attract a new woman. I'd have lots of customers but I'd also have my work cut out for me, that's for sure.

I suspect that many of them, entering the online dating scene because of divorce or the death of a long-term spouse, are one-woman guys. They somehow managed to persuade some innocent young thing to marry them, back in the days when lust was paramount and subtlety wasn't required but those days have well and truly gone. As with the dancing scene, time has passed and things have changed. The women they're hoping to attract have mostly come out of long-term relationships. If they're like me, they know what they want and they aren't prepared to put up with infantile nonsense from men who should know better.

My first piece of advice to would-be suitors, you ask? Just tell it how it is. Don't try to gild the somewhat aged, wilting lily. You're not twenty-five any more and no sensible woman expects you to behave as if you are. Let the lady of your dreams decide how handsome or young-at-heart you are and whether your sense of humour meshes with hers. Hopefully she's reasonably mature and if she's the right one, she'll love you anyway, whatever your shortcomings.

Anyway, in spite of my clever advice to others, I'm feeling a wee bit discouraged about it all. Still, after another week or two, I've been to coffee and dinner and the movies with several very pleasant men, and I'm exchanging emails with two others who present possibilities. There are new contenders for the title of Mr Wonderful popping up on both sites every day, so perhaps I shouldn't give up hope just yet. What I have to do, I guess, is to have faith. I need to keep telling myself that there's someone out there who's just right for me. I'll let you know when I find him, or when he finds me, if I live that long.

Nina Ritchie

After having moved to the Whittlesea area in 2017, I decided to join U3A creative writing in search of some sort of course that would stimulate my brain a little!

That certainly happened with this group. I had not put pen to paper for over thirty five years since my university days. Needless to say, I found it quite difficult at first, but with the help and inspiration I have derived from the sharing of ideas and listening to the stories that emanate from the other members of my group, I am starting to think about topics to write about.

I hope to construct some more short stories in the near future.

Cleopatra brought to life

Short Story

For as long as I can remember I've carried a curious fascination for Queen Cleopatra, The last Pharaoh of Egypt.

The attraction has been fueled by the classic movies of the Hollywood era. My imagination would run wild with Exotic scenes of a beautiful Elizabeth Taylor cast as Cleopatra, with her lover Marc Antony played by the handsome Richard Burton. Visions of a Colorful Egyptian barge floating down the river Nile with the backdrop of Pyramids, Palm Trees and giant Sphinxes. The two actors locked in an embrace with slaves on either side them, fanning them with big Palm leaves.

This version is the Cleopatra of my childhood, the one who, up until recently, in my mind, was a majestic woman of beauty and charm! That is until I started to do some research into the documented history of her complex and tumultuous life.

It is said that the story of Cleopatra has been interpreted in many ways over hundreds of years. At worst She has been portrayed as an evil scheming woman who would stop at nothing to keep the throne of Egypt, even if it involved murdering all of her siblings. At best She was a highly educated and astute Politician who aligned herself with the most powerful figures of the time in order to hold onto power in her region and improve Egypt's position.

Indeed there is also doubt cast as to whether she was a great beauty. Some images depicted of her found on ancient Egyptian coins aren't so flattering. But unless she comes to life before our eyes, all history relating to her, is subject to personal interpretation.

In portraying this narrative, I like to think of Cleopatra as one of the most powerful and influential women of ancient times, who, from a very early age was groomed to be a leader of an empire by her father. She was well educated and taught by the best scholars of the time. The young Cleopatra mastered several languages and no doubt developed many skills that she would call upon in years to come, not only for her survival but that of her children and her beloved Egypt.

So I would like to take you back to the year 30BC, Queen Cleopatra is around 39 years old and I have been granted a personal audience with her.

The following few questions are what I would ask if this encounter really did come true:

"Queen Cleopatra, It is such an honor to meet you. Never in my wildest dreams would I have imagined to be seated opposite one of the ancient worlds most powerful women. "

"What a turbulent and eventful life you have led. You have seen so many of your relatives murdered for the throne of Egypt and you are the last remaining sibling, apart from your own children. How do you come to terms with all the bloodshed that has occurred over the year's?"

" I was taught from an early age that this was the Ptolomey way of life! Yes I have witnessed horrible events. But from when I was a little girl, my father Pharaoh Ptolomey X11, had to groom me in a manner that would make me resilient in the face of chaos! The Roman Empire has been the superpower in control of the ancient world for many years. Egyptians have had to live under the rule of Rome and survive."

"My father knew that my brothers and myself would ultimately have the responsibility of being the last Pharaohs of Egypt. He had no choice but to toughen me up. But in doing so, he also gave me the best education that one could receive! So along with all the bad things I was exposed to, I was able to harness all those wonderful things I was taught over the years, to ensure my survival. "

"Queen Cleopatra you aligned yourself politically and romantically with two of the most powerful men in the Roman Empire in order to preserve the throne and your country. I ask you did you have any love for these men or were they merely an instrument in your plan."

" Not in the beginning, I needed them both politically, but I came to love and respect the Great Cesar's intellect as I am certain he loved mine. He was initially not so easily led. I had to use every power I had in me, both physically and mentally to win him over and gain his trust. This is where my years of study came into play. Once I won him over with my intellect, the seduction process came easily, he was a man after all and I gave him a son as a reward for returning me to the Throne of Egypt.

"Excuse me for a moment, but can I ask you Queen Cleopatra is it true that you had yourself rolled up in a carpet and bought into Caesar's Chamber. "

"That of course is a common myth, in reality Caesar would not have allowed a foreign article to enter his chamber for fear of being murdered! But it does make a good story. In reality I made my own way to him. "

"Sorry to have sidetracked you with that question, but I was merely pointing out to those that will read this article today, that history can be confusing and how the lines can be blurred between reality and legend!"

"Can we get back to your now husband Marc Antony, do you love him. We know that the Romans do not acknowledge your relationship as he already has a wife.''

"We are detested in Rome. They call our relationship a "sham"

The Romans have always scorned me, I have been resented from the time I started my affiliation with Caesar. They could not come to terms with the fact that a woman could have so much influence over the most powerful men of The Empire."

"Of course my association with Marc Antony started as political. We needed each other. He required an alliance with Egypt both financially and strategically to fund his battles. I needed him as a protectorate to hold on to the throne but It didn't take long for us to become lovers. Our physical attraction just happened naturally.

Actually, I have more in common with him than I ever had with Caesar. You must have heard that we are renown for our passion and revelry, much to the disgust of the Roman people."

"But I now fear the end is near for our alliance! Marc Antony has been defeated in Parthia. The Roman senate about to strip him of his title and Octavian has denounced Egypt and declared war on me. I must plan my exit strategy! "

"What do you mean your Majesty!"

"I cannot be humiliated by Octavian, for he will have me shamed and remove my throne, for all of Rome and Egypt to witness therefore I must now enter the next World in glory. All will be revealed soon! Marc Antony's fate is sealed and so is mine!"

Queen Cleopatra, I Thank your time and will ask no more of you as I know that your legend will live on for centuries, but I beg of you to just give one last reflection on your life that is how do you want to be remembered by future generations."

"People will form their own opinion of me but I have always known what I must do to align myself with the God's. I know what I have achieved in my lifetime and have done for my beloved Egypt and its subjects. I do not have any regrets, I was born to be a Queen and I will die as one.''

Her name is Ezra.

Short Story

She stands there covered from head to toe in the traditional black abayat. This is the dress code that the country she comes from demand that all women wear who dare go out in the community.

Of course, what stands out about her is the eyes. That is the only bit of her body that is not concealed. They are electric blue. One has only to look closely to tell they are the eyes of a young woman. Bright, clear, still full of passion and idealism.

That is all you can distinguish of her, she looks the same as all the other women young and old that scurry around the busy market place bartering or buying groceries for their families.

In public places she has no identity, She cannot attract undue attention from the opposite sex. An anonymous dark cloaked figure, a non-entity.

But one has only to look through the slits of the veiled burqa to imagine what kind of a woman is under all that cloth. A vibrant and extremely, striking individual. What is the saying "the eyes are a window to the soul"!

No you cannot hide those qualities if you look at her eyes! She does not yet realize that men do stare at her. They fantasize about what lies under that dark cloak. That is the irony of the situation, when you cannot see someone in the flesh your imagination cuts in!

Ezra makes her way hastily down the narrow dusty side streets of the city to her home. It is not good for a young woman to stay out for very long without a chaperone. Her mother will fret! What would people say about the family, the shame!

The door to the house opens as the key turns the lock. Her mother stands at the door relieved that she has made it home quickly, but as soon as Ezra is in the door and it is closed, the headpiece comes off. She shakes her silky raven black hair that runs past her shoulders. Yes she is indeed a beautiful girl! High cheekbones, full lips and yes those blue almond shaped eyes. A sigh of relief leaves her lips. In the sanctity of her home this girl can be herself, an individual, a free spirit, full of life and love. At least until the she is allowed to venture out again and turn into another nameless female figure that you see frequenting the streets of Kabul.

The Table has been set

Short Story

The table has been set with a *wonderous* array of food. What an assortment of *delicious* morsels to behold. There are little cakes with *blue*, *yellow* and green icing. Then there are plates of tiny little sandwiches all lined up in a row. There are also little meat pies staked up high like a pyramid.

She circles around the table so she can *peruse* every inch of the offering. Her *mind* is only focused on one thing, that food on the table. She starts *calculating* the distance between the edge of the table and the first plate on offer. She shifts her *gaze* towards the plate of party pies to the left., looks around to see if anyone is present. The coast is clear. She attempts to make her attack.

Up goes her chest so it is at table level. She reaches out and makes a grab for the party pies. She pulls the plate towards her. Bang, Crash, it lands on the ground, her face is buried in amongst the pies. She has a startled look on her face and then she hears a screech from the Kitchen.

Oh my goodness! Caught out, but by this stage she has already gobbled three pies. What a sight to behold. Pieces of china and meat pie strewn from one end of the floor to the other. Her face is covered with evidence that she is the culprit, she has bits of pie stuck to it. "Oops", she thinks to herself, "I am in deep shit I have been caught out, what will my punishment be! Will I be banished for the rest of the day to the backyard, or will she take pity on me and just scold me and let it pass". She sits up and awaits the final decision with eyes cast down and tail between her legs.

Her mistress rushes over and quickly surveys the situation. On one hand she wants to laugh out loud because the scenario looks *hilarious*.

She realises that it is partly her fault as she left the table unattended while the one track minded "Hungarian Vizler" was in the vicinity. She cannot bring herself to banish her for the rest of the afternoon. So what will the punishment be? She has to act fast or else Ellie will forget what has happened and move on to the next mishap! "Bad girl, look what you've done, what I am I going to do with you? Out you go to the backyard"!

Ellie sleeks off, head down in shame, tail between her legs. "That's it she thinks to herself I'm gone I am going to have spend all afternoon out here while they eat all that food, there will be no chance to get some scraps now. Oh well, I will see if Master takes pity on me and lets me back up. Look there he is, clearing the yard, I'll just go over and make him feel sorry for me being stuck outside, so he will open the gate and I can go back up. That won't be too hard, I don't think he knows what I've done"!

Her Mistress looks down from the balcony and watches Ellie skillfully try and get her master's attention. Oh what a clever girl she is, but it's always about food. That's how her one track mind works. She cant stay mad at her and proceeds to clean up the mess on the floor. Once the guests arrive and settle down she will let her back up again and allow her to weave that "magic" charm on them so they will feed her bits of food. That's okay, all is forgiven, Ellie is just a Dog after all!

Paul Hollander

 1 9 6 9 / 7 0 P a u l
H o l l a n d e r
J u n i o r
T r a d e s m a n
N o r t h W a l e s U K

Paul Hollander was born in England, Royal Tunbridge Wells Kent. Left home at 16 years old joined the Junior Tradesman Regiment in North Wales, he became the best recruit of regiment 1969/70 Kinmel Park in Bodelwyddan.

He delivered poetry and prose, discovered in the virginal essence of falling in, out of love. At 16 years old, passion overflowed; expressing his feelings to paper helped him perceive a vista of a dance between his heart, mind and spirit. Commenting; the pen is mightier than the sword and much kinder.
1974, at 20 years old Paul followed one of his dreams, travelled across-land to Australia where he has lived ever since, remarking; as soon as I arrived in Perth WA, it was as if I had returned home.

1977 he journeyed by himself across Europe to North Africa, Egypt, travelled south to South Africa, 6500 km. It was during this 5-month experience that nearly cost him his life, twice over; horrific encounters that truly crystallised the notion; the pen is mightier than the sward quoted many times in his memoir he is collating.
Paul adheres to the philosophy; Letting everything be your teacher, and as he got older conveniently adopts; You are never too old to be young.
Retired (RN) Registered General and Psychiatric Nurse; specialised in Drug and Alcohol (dual diagnosis); Forensic Nursing; Dip: Counselling; Dip: HRM
Now 66 years young,   he enjoys the challenge of Toastmasters (public speaking) Bushwalking, camping helps him celebrate the reverence of mother nature, away from bustles of big cities and lights.
Pauls passion for writing has intensified since retiring, experimenting with types of genres in literature. He continues to celebrate narratives that journey beyond veils of so-called death and rejoices the notion; WE finish with new beginnings... smiling to himself as he opens a bottle of red merlot; would you care for a drink? He is cheeky, his cheekiness carries a defensive smile that invites; a calm peace and serenity. Sub-textually, surprises await the reader.
Paul has enclosed four abridged versions of his latest work;
My Fortunate Life
In the Shadow of a Ghost Gum
Deliverance... Returned to Sender
When the Warmth of Death Is Sweeter Than Life
Contact Details: Paulhollander@hotmail.com

'You Are Never Too Old To Be Young'

Memoir

Larapinta 2017

A fortunate life

Not to brag about it, but I sang with a member of ABBA!
How fortunate is that?

Hi,
I'm Paul Hollander
Welcome

If you want to read something strait-laced, you're barking up the wrong tree.

Find another tree, bark to your heart's content.

I present to you, fragments of my ~~unfortunate~~ fortunate life.

A mosaic to write. As I do in U3A Creative Writing Group.

Or talk as I do in U3A (Tutor) Listening to your story.

Do you have stories waiting to be read?

Don't wait long. You might miss your chance to sing your song.
Did you ask me... how long is a piece of string?
I don't know... don't care.
Forget the piece of the string, unless you can convert it to a wick for
enlightening.
They have compared the protective sequencing at the end of a genetic
sequence [telomeres] to the continually decreasing wicks... time-
bomb fuse, bang, finito.
Just what you wanted to know!
You can borrow my light until I burn my fingers.

In the Flare of a Match
Let me strike a matchstick on my existence!
Once I was temperamental, volatile, not any more... you're safe and
sound.
I suggest you don't read the next few pages, you might get your
fingers burnt.
Maybe, the other hand, can light your wick at the same time?
We can become light-workers-thinkers of fashion together.

I even have a few matches left, if you're reading this so do you, so
much fun.
Yes, where were you, Paul.?
I was pretending to be a ghost... jumping up in the air.

Can you see me?

Captured Moments PDH - Infinity

Soon I shall be 66 years old. I'm not a ghost.
Did I hear you say:
Paul! You're never too old to be young.

As mentioned, I belong to the group, called ABBA:
My surname is Hollander, doesn't sound Swedish, but I'm willing to go Dutch.
I'm not about to sing SOS, because I haven't much Money Money Money;
But we will be fruitful for knowing each other: Knowing Me Knowing you... AHA!
Paulhollander@hotmail.com.au
Ageing Baby Boomers in Australia (ABBA)
Baby boomer cohort - the 5.5 million people born between 1946 and 1965.
Bryan Mc Nally (ABBA) Paul Hollander (ABBA) sang together: 'Morning Has Broken.'
Reminiscing, remember when those... school and church days.
Bryan and Paul confessing to adoring songs from Pink Floyd; particular song Brain Damage From The Dark Side of the Moon (1973)

On 'The Bright Side Of The Moon' (2016) I'm a proud member of The University Of The Third Age (U3A)

It might sound like I'm going crazy. Who cares...?

My wife has enjoyed my songs for the last 40 years. Sometimes my better half, is half deaf, don't know why? Selective hearing?
In our 'Creative Writing Group,' we have many stars, moons, and planets.
One twinkling star hates using the words Old Age. So we call ourselves the Third Age.
What does that mean? Ask our group.

Whatever you say don't mention Old Age.

Okay, I shall try to be ~~desperately~~ serious.
By now, you should be thinking to yourselves; who is this nutcase
Paul Hollander?
Well, I'm a macadamia nut by self-design.
Work the rest out for yourself
You will find me sweet, others a bloody pain in the butt. That's okay.
I'm a kernel without rank or title, just planting myself, here and there.
Just Paul,
A motivator of people.
My premise:
You're Never Too Old To Be Young.
This is my serious look of contemplation.

Portland Victoria 2017
I hadn't been to the toilet in 5 days. Can you tell?
Self-deprecating helps me confront to trim any simmering pride.
Reminds me, the job ain't finished until someone does the paperwork
is an old mantra... manta stingray!

Born In Royal Tunbridge Wells Kent, England, 1953
[Royalty runs through my veins, but that's a secret]

As a kid, The River Thames UK. was my floating backyard.

We lived in a Jewish hotel attic for ten years: two adults and four
children; two-rooms; three small windows; no toilet or water; the
bathroom one storey below; one shared water tap; hotel located
200m from the River Thames. My backyard harboured boats and
yachts that slept lopsided on grey mud, waiting for the dark
awakening sea.

My playground beach amazed me with its constant shifting seashore.
The sea played with the sand, uncovering various coloured stones,
coins, sometimes bullets. Oodles, of puddled mud, with hairy seaweed
and smelly dead fish when the tide was out. The sea commanded by
the moon with its invisible influences delivered windy king tides: on
occasions causing boats to break anchor, hulls crushed apart by the
breakwaters for me to salvage. Dangerous for an excited young
beachcomber called Paul, a drifter, a daydreamer of mosaics.
I could relate to my one-eyed teddy bear whose eye was hanging from
a thread
As a child, trying to understand an echoing notion; I'm not supposed
to be here [world] infuriated my mom, no end, life was scary and
disjointed. I was eight years old.
Word imagery and imagination, delivered by nature, gave me an inner
world full of visual comforts.
As a little man, I was introvert and tactile. Touching pebbles, sand,
seaweed, driftwood, old bottles, bones and leaves gave me an
extended presence, passing by; drifting in a bottle? Smaller worlds I
could relate to, like my one-eyed teddy bear, whose eye was hanging
from a thread. This thread I could read as being poignant, another
big word I didn't understand but felt, evoking a keen sense of sadness
followed by joy when the teddy's eyes were pinpoint and fixed with
another new eye, my world was looking up, up to the heavens.

I felt trapped like a message in a bottle to nowhere; 'Mum, I want to return where I came from.' Mum was wordless and dismayed. 'What am I going to do with you, Paul?'

I loved my parents but feared my father. He doubted I belonged to him. They proved him wrong. He never apologised or reimburse money as he promised, I wonder why? Father was a fantastic storyteller, mother always smiled as we travelled through the story, as if she was part-parcel, a silent presence in waiting. Father was a hard-worker. One income. With tempers that terrified me. I peed myself, that also frightened me. I use to think; even my little silly willy cries. I can still recall trickling warmth in my undies, overflowing down my inner thigh, absorbed into my socks before filling my shoes.

I'll never forget the sound of squelching pee in my shoes.

Father seldom drank alcohol or went out. Can never recollect going on holiday as a family. We never owned a car. Father was dyslexic. Cannot remember any books or reading matter in our home; seeing my parent read was foreign. Beano and Dandy comics I recall. Pictured: war heroes, flowers, animals, cars, boat cigarette cards acted as a portal to other dynamic, often scary worlds. The world of nature, my companion, grounded a balance within me that now harvest stories about seasons weathered through my pen.

Where did I come from? Why am I here? Where do we go when we die?

My poor reading, writing antagonised my teachers the first year at high school. An English teacher took me under his wing, fed me books until I could fly. Poetic connections took flight cultivating my inner world of bookworms, cocoons and butterflies. But little about death; nobody wanted to go there? How strange, how curious?

Consumed with surging male hormones, experienced steadfast lapses of reason. Pink Floyd was teaching me to fly, different from my beloved school teacher. My inner world imaginings were spawning. Like The Great Barrier reef coral. Each week was a full moon,

offering high tides, overflowing with new discoveries. Flight of ideas
feed my thoughts and feelings floated to the surface with complex
scripts await understanding:
What is the ultimate purpose of our existence?
No answer convinced me: You're too young to ask such questions
was no answer. That made me think; was I, old wine in a young bottle.
Visible to me now, they just didn't understand my vintage. I remained
bottled up and confused with the first impression. Visualising adults
facial expressions, as if constipated when answering me.

Space between my pen-nib and paper. A world to escape. I called it
my synaptic imaginings. Picture a pen in hand poised one millimetre
above paper, a gap exists. Focus within the gap. Ponder, then decode
thoughts and feelings that melt… flow from pen nib swimming onto
paper: a tadpole spellbound, morphing ideas, exuding nothing into
something. What a picture! As if my pen was a telescope, retrieving
wonderful subterranean dream time. On occasions, gut-wrenching
with a black dog abyss. I always retreated within my bottle for safety
rumination and reconciliation.

As a teenager of the1960s, Enigma was my name. My world rained
images. Bob Dylan sang about me, of all people! Believing I was a
leaf blowing in the wind; metaphors;
His voice was music to my ears and analogies; What strings are to
guitar, love is to life.
Living on housing trust estate, the outskirt of London, you had to be as
tough as nails.
I didn't rust out just-rusted-within, a rustic fertile soil cultivated a
nuance of self-understanding. Sometimes self-loathing rode me, like
John Wayne, into the ground, with the black dog nipping at my heels
and spurs on my rump.
I couldn't spell, 'impartiality' let alone believe in 'it' as a concept.
'Mods (scooter riders) and Rockers (motorbike riders) of the '60s

~~didn't give a tink~~er's cuss. Simon and Garfunkel's duo cared. They
offered a bleeder like me a: Bridge Over Troubled Water. But alas,
being like a leaf in the wind finding solace wasn't easy, being legless.
Attached to a branch of society fearing being blown to smithereens in
a nuclear war uprooted me, before getting rooted was a devastating
notion to grapple with.

My name was Hollander, not Smithereens. Until ruminations echoed;
Would you rather be a hammer than a nail? Nested like a precious
egg in my heart. I didn't enjoy being tough as nails or hard-boiled,
nor the fragility of being crushed with yolk on my face. Humour was
ironic, a hot iron spun around one's head, much like the nail and
hammer impacting each other together. What a choice? Much like
life, living to die, dying to live hammered home facts of life. Learning
by mistakes without becoming bent wasn't easy. Hold nails between
forefinger and thumb trusting your friend to hit the nail not my thumb
was not funny; just a cruel joke, everyone laughing except my bloody
thumb and bruised pride.

Early puberty, I fell in love with a gorgeous girl named Dawn; she
was my sunshine. I wanted to give her my heart, then realised I
would be heartless. I was emotionally dumbfounded. My tongue, tied
and twisted, nailed, to my desk, shackled with love. Then, I broke
anchor, navigated a drifting heart, that penned my compass soul into
the heavenly clouds, hoping to see my divine Dawn. She was an
angel. I was dreaming once again.
Sad though, I never experienced my mortal dawn.
Dawn never accepted my heart. She didn't believe in suicide. Launch
me into troubled waters, I couldn't swim. Only her fading sunset
viewed from a Bridge Over Troubled Water saved my life from
drowning in tears. My heart slithered, morphed as an octopus into
the bottle; contorted, contemplating life and death; parallel to the gap
between the hammer and the nail. I released my sacred [holy] heart to

the great stream of consciousness, sinking into deep uncharted waters, believing I'll never look at another sunrise the same brilliant way without blinding myself. I would be Paul on the road to Damascus asking;

Dawn, Dawn, why dost thou harbour my heart and soul?
I held my breath for eighteen months until becoming blue in the face. My old mate, octopus (self-talk) offered me a blood transfusion and one of its three hearts, in exchange for being released. I accepted, freeing myself from the shackles of love. Strange, Dawn had an awakening! She contacted me several years too late. Our identities had changed several times in as many years. My Dawn had melted like butter on toast, still tantalising and hot. I never looked her square in her eyes, in fear of gaining an appetite and getting toasted. I confess to thinking about what a way to die.

Alongside Bob Dylan and my two heart Octopus. Not to forget the occasional 10 tablets of sennokot (for constipation). Being self-deprecating, usually considered a good trait, a quality of someone with a wry sense of humour. I once confused self-deprecating with self-defaecating, I near shit myself in embarrassment. Like Tony Abbott leader of the Australian Liberal party, hand me a tissue blooper: suppository of wisdom.

My phoenix of time approaches threescore years and ten. That's cool, I guess.
Unlike migrating birds that suffer starvation and exhaustion. At 66, a retired Registered General Nurse (RN) and Registered Psychiatric Nurse (RPN). I've finally come of age. Hallelujah, Leonard Cohen sang for me. Entering the University Of The Third Age (U3A). Energised with a sense of emancipation, not constipation, as some might think, and that's okay. To share my five senses orbiting the wonders of mother nature that continue to astound and impress me, to bleed my words: as a bleeder in flight that enthrones his phoenix of experiences into a quill: scratched out nestle thoughts, feelings, ideas

and belief incubated by life interaction. 2020 I shall publish a book, titled; When The Warmth Of Death Is Sweeter Than Life, followed into a theatre play, that has financial backing.

A phoenix's quill teased by the inkpot, resting on its rim
Reflections of my life are fading illusions that mimic puddles in the sun. With bottled up allusions. Sometimes I wonder about sensory perception cocktails.
Mixed delusions can entertain if you don't take yourself too seriously.
My inner octopus (self-talk) has pent up ink. The ink-cap is part open.
A phoenix's quill teased by the inkpot, resting on its rim of time, poised, offering a billing account.

To write meaningful words; What do you mean Paul?
As with sleepwalking comes varying degrees of awakenings that have their say through different yawn breaths of life. Entranced words following periodical shades of passion filter through my sole domain, to percolate; to entice a thirst. I subscribe to.
Do I write?
It remains my choice. Try not breathing, how long did you last?
Awakenings continue to be my seasonal buddy. Budding leaves…
flows, blossom falls.
Temperament ebbs and flows succinctly with a conceivable tide of my tapering existence.
A contrast of inspirations I've learned to live with. To be my seasonal friend, to embrace. Personal joy (within) and happiness (without) gauged by the depth of its own sadness, elicits an emotional response, pirouettes contentment.
A soft voice whispers for the entire world to… overhear.

Neither joy nor sadness can exist alone, but coexist;

Living in appreciation of each other, offering a comparison, a duality,
a currency to exchange with the authentic love of acceptance,
shadowed by none judgement.
Much like a coined-heart on its axis, spinning a face of joy, followed
by a face of sadness.
That centralises one face of coexistence, an expression of evolving
contentment.
Billions of micro-worlds revolving on a macro-world within our solar
system.
You're never too old to be young,
My humble offering to you; the currency of my Heart, Soul and Spirit.

Pauls poetry and more...

Tulip fever 2017

✦★✧☙🙖✧★✦

In The Shadow Of A Ghost Gum

Poetry: An Abridge Version
Branch One Of Seven Branches
Will publish in 2020

Captured Moments by Paul Hollander

Branch One
Tree Spirits Escort My Way

Whenever I become engrossed,
especially with matters of nature,
I resonate an inner glow.

Entering a beautiful world of contemplation,
metaphors fall awake within.
Imagineering takes form.
Within the shadow of a Ghost,
I dreamt a dream.
Within that dream,
I become cocooned.

Blissful state inside quivers rebirth.
A leaf in motion, untethered,
hugging a silky web cocoon,
impermanence in transit.

To awakening a joyous flutter within life.
Wind beneath wings, surfing dust-beams,
while mother earth hovers below.
Gliding within clouds of mystery forms
radiant light offering...
shades of sleep.

Sprays of shade danced in a rainbow mist.
Winged free... instinctive freedom
a compass castaway
pinned from the heart of love.

Tree Spirits Escort My Way.
Trees standing upright,
lurching gait sway in the light wind.
Branches outstretched,
beholding pockets of vapour.
Entities from the earth–girted thighs,
rooted below, danced entwined
creep as ghost silkworms casting their spell,
dispelling the myths of hell.

Clustered dualities, being and doing
merge an embrace.
Silent loving grace
moans silently rooted without haste
Bathed moist stirrings, birth in natures mist...
Seven tree shadows awake a flicker.
Fanning silhouettes
a rustling puppet show.
Leaves move imagination.
Furrowed Brow
dries anticipation impressed.
Tree Spirits Escort My Way.
Orchestrated branches play Bach concordance.
Light strings maneuverer from heavens hand stretch torch.

Yawning movements captured in misty delights.
Captures a glimpse of a ballet dancer in the dark.
How strange, how perfect, this ageless image?
Mystical wood-wind instruments utter inter-being,
engulfed in steamy enlightened curtains showed;
tree puppets in tune, sway string ensemble,
crowned from the heavens.
Perceived stage performance,
between tree shadows, branched handed several dim hazes.
Performing games with shafts of darting lights,
shepherd into a state of an imagined swim.
as if accompanied by a human swan,
her ambience, her ball.
Swims into an absence, as if a Seance recalls.
Perceived unknowing, feeling light-headed,
disorientated but bemused strange joy.

Tree Spirits Escort My Way.
The ambience within the moments,
bewilderment – a shift in mood,
drifts the timeline within being in change.
Struggled breath,
fearful at first.
Fish flapping out of water,
caught, reeled in by a silver beam of light,
towards an unassuming tree harbour.
Transformed into a promising loving presence;
tall, comprehensive and still.
A spectacular Ghost Gum magnetised an attraction.
Sporting a perfect silvery-grey skin,
smooth satin bark with groaning sounds,
resonate with its neighbours immersive in
a celebration in time.

Tree Spirits Escort My Way
Open heartstrings strobe an anchorage
to a beat of love and affection.
Pulsing songs through the mist,
serenading orphans seeds,
in search of a lock, a home.

Keys, to an imaginary stairway.
Heaven.
Unlocked each step in tune.
Shafts of finger-light, shimmering a lake's surface sun,
underscore rippling notes,
Rainbow vibes flow out... a web in the breeze.
Harpsichords, escort my nature,
guided by a ghost gum human swan.
Music notes (leaves) dancing like confetti stars
encompass unconditional acceptance,
without judgment, upon a carpet,
path by leaves for tomorrows sustenance.
Offering a marriage without a bride.
Antique tree rings, formed from their sacred crown to girth.
Tree rings of old, escort my way ringing in my ears.

Surrounded by ancient Ghost Gums whispering, how wonderful,
thy art they love branched out like arms.

An opening chorus follows a beacon baton,
A spiritual wand that ponders the question,
who is this ghostly human swan?

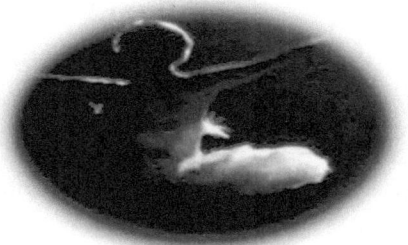

Captured Moments PDH

Tree Spirits Escort My Way.
✦★✦♧♤★✦✦

When The Warmth Of Death Is Sweeter Than Life

An Extract Poem:
Proposed: Audiobook, Book; Play. To be published in 2020.

'Our bittersweet Bee - Our sweet memories'

A love song
(By the late: Eadie & Godfrey Goodwood)
Godfrey —(((((((:))))— Eadie
Joy Blooms Contentment

Prelude

One week before our leaving [vacating our bodies] we both experienced
concurrent dreams we share with you
Our paralleled dreams composed into one love song (Poem)
(They lay engulfed within their precious Forget-Me-Nots flowers:
Epitomise their stream of true love consciousness.)
These Forget-Me-Nots flowers harmonise our love song;
Goodbye Forget-Me-Nots… my sweet, will always be
The orchestra of
Birds
Bees
Insects
Tweet – Hum

A LOVE SONG
FROM
Godfrey ~~(((((((:))))~~ Eadie
Joy Blooms Contentment
****

Together we are... Still... no more'.
Our bittersweet Bee - Our sweet memories

'Begged of you my love, as you asked of me, remember never to forget
Forget-Me-Nots that stemmed our wedding rings for eternity'.

'We both held those petaled flowers, with whispering wings,
hummed with a breeze with such ease'.

'We knelt upon the moving lemongrass, as autumn leaves played in
the breeze'.
'Natures confetti, breezed colour through our hair floating effortless
free'.

'We exchanged bold gold wedding rings, restored from the
stems of Forge-Me-Nots:
One small and One large shimmering ring.
'Bold gold will see us old, we whispered; prey holy'.
'Remember, we cried with joy as we devoted a heartthrob song to
each other'.

'If the time comes, when we cease to feel; heal one-another as
we try to knell'.
'Remember, those moist warm breaths we exchanged, as we listened
to inner whispers from our hearts... ring echo resonates our soul's
bell toil.

'Our tongues entwined a knot in time to live for each other
beyond time.

'Never' will not keep us apart, never will follow us together'.

*'Wind-winged feathers of doves carried us beneath loving breaths of
fairies.*

*We are presents for each other, to unwrap a crown for each, born
unique, breathe not, but live; with a Universal pulse forever'.*

Our bittersweet Bee - Our sweet memories

'Timed wedding rings worn thin, borne witness to scorn and
thorn endured survived punctures, ring true our love secured'.

*'No more fearing the fear of saying; 'Goodbye my love'. We had to
die while we have time on our side; to die a planned death succinct
together; dead on time. With the want of two hearts, one thought
filled the mind, we speak from deep well-being souls.*

'We crown ourselves from birth, We crowned ourselves to
sleep now we wake no more the yawn of life that creeps'.

'We are on the other side of life where death ceases to live.

*A door lay open; our bodies lay asleep for us to leave. To leaving
behind an earthiness of age to return to the soil of earth forwarded
frailty we give away and say good-ridden'.*

'How times flies. 'Together, we have flown from being doves
in love to being angels of love'.

*'I still feel your caring hand secure, my natural cure. You never let go
my love!*

*Your reassuring smile. Your cheeks glance a cheeky grin a new day;
as if we are young over once again.*

Look, my dear, my hands are free of arthritis and deformity'.

'We have no wrinkles nor papery skin to tear or write complaints. Heard your heartbeat write glory hallelujah, your breath resuscitates a new life, a new world. Once a younger version, pastime, place, and person in time how quick, as our Willow body wilted overnight; a dream without any screams'.

Once upon a dream, we had fallen awake in love. Heads in the sky were floating a heavenly kite. We rolled with the years, played in the cloud shade, and drank lemonade sweet as bubbles tickled noses – sneezed while attempting to seize the sun'.

Our bittersweet Bee - Our sweet memories

'When Death Became Warmer Than the Sweetness of Life … Joy had lost its buoyancy - Suffering daily survival was such a drain'.

Two hearts, one mind, we refused to part. We tore life's script apart. We did it our way as we planned from the start. Start with a new forward when our old parts fell apart. Nourishment of music feeds our souls pure, courage to see a life-end a cure'.

'Comforted by whisperings violin strings, Cellos gave us a base, with ample space. Never to fret only hear-see forests winds whistling marram grass. Dancing whiskers in dunes of time - rain melody ingrains as if in a monsoon hiding above clouds a Blue Moon.

With worlds of sands running through our fingers and toes. Utterings squeaking souls as we walked, the language of intimacy. Magnify our insight; sparkling worlds divide. Tangible; intangible abilities worked in shadow ingrained with kindness bonded our incline".

'We gazed within a myriad of miracle seeds: as grains that pulse a life unique; ignited seasoned gain with a rain of love conceived, baptised in the light. We grinned wisely as snakes losing their first season skin; born a new body through motion steered our spirit hearts and minds free.

Warm icicle drips sparkling crystals that hold dazzling coloured stars in space. We spied kaleidoscope colours bursting rainbows suns delight'.

'Celebrated colours with fragrances of summer rain mixed cut hay and lavender. An offering closes at hand, to touch, to taste a melody without pain, without swelling. A notion of the wellbeing beyond one's past earthly boots. Enabled once more; a cobbler of souls, beyond souls of the earth, exampled by a Special-One who walked on water leading the way home'.

Our bittersweet Bee - Our sweet memories

'No need to walk with pressured distraught haste, especially for water's sake. We lounge a design; a spectacular sunrise that orbit sunsets in one sleepy blink. Fallen awake with happy familiar faces, once discrete, out of sight (deceased love ones) now appeared with a torch of light. A tone of togetherness harmonised by the Son. The one who walked on water day and night with the sun of day moon at night. No darkness, no shadows, only togetherness, felt right'.

'Remember we begged each, as a blushing bride/groom never to surrender until we die? We gave each other Forget-Me-Nots, a token of true love eternal. Mime together, never, never, never until we die together than live on forever as seeds of loving flowers.
We shielded ourselves each other against unimaginable pain and untold suffering. Towards the end of life, we chose death as opposed to prolonged dying cost each dearly.
Instead, inevitable death found us live life again without body into spirit form of light'.

'Grains of sand spoke invisible worlds in every grain of sand, symbolic of stars above. Wild-flowers talked about the invisible heavens in the heart of every flower; a residence within every grain of sand'.

'Darling, you're still the delicate of blooms, my blossom bee eternal. You have held me to your bosom free, a wildflower in the summer sun - you opened for me to come to thee. As I to you in a loving embrace, treasured mindful moments, it's not a race; you are holding each other's Ace.

Heavenly moments they are embedded — rippled memories on golden beaches, afar for sure. Under Divine eyes; universal stars winking; 'it's right'.

Gods saw us creating upon Celestial Grain of Sand; momentarily were Gods.

'We planted our earthly wedding rings of commitment. Gold spheres are containing our hearts supreme without fears. Yesterday seeds for tomorrow season harvest. Blessed by the light of love. We are, in part, earthly seeds. Inconceivable worlds in trillions of grains of sand with trillions of flowers waiting for budding expressions of love.

Dreams Have Ending

Godfrey —(((((((:)))— Eadie

Joy Blooms Contentment

Eadie and Godfrey looked into each other's eyes

breathed as one love,

IN

Silence, Space and Stillness

They partner as one tongue

A Poem Song Parted

In Love

Captured Moments By PDH

Godfrey ((((((((:)))) Edie

✦★✱&🙰★★✦

Deliverance:

Play: (An Abridge Version)

The Bare Threads Of Love
ACT One
Honeymooner's
Agate & Athena

Captured Moments PDH

'Agate, can you see those beautiful white Angels...?
I genuinely believe their existence allow our being together!
It was a miracle, was it not?
Just thinking about it sends waves of shivers down my spine...
dripping icicles as frozen teardrops that have no eyes to see, only a
shrouded dark veil that separated you and me.
You must never go there, my love... promise me. Promise me please'.

    'Athena, I shall always kiss you goodnight and kiss your cheeks
    good morning, and hold you tight.

'Hold me my dearest, squeeze me, warm me from death's breath that
haunts me so. Condensation that still speaks without form condemns
you... As though you are dead, frozen, captured within rigour-mortise.
Protect me from its cold, condescending eyeless shroud offering
teardrops that have no sight, nor insight. Only dormancy dancing

with shadows.

Promise me... never leave me alone again to shadow-box the shadows of death!'.

Agate held Athena in his secure arms, squinting as he squeezed loving warmth into Athena's shivering body. Comfort and reassurance were an act of her daily needs: mopping tailings of morbid mortal aftermath since Agate, rescued, returned home. She closes her eyes as a child finds comfort from a mother's breast. Then feeling complete, breathes residual of despair; more out of habit than reality. With a sigh of relief, her breathing and pulse return to normal. Looked into Agate's eyes, Athena sees oceans that offers a life-raft for two, floating on love, not death

ACT Two
Ponderous Worlds Depicted As-One

Captured Moments PDH

As a marine biologist, Agate was in his glory habituating such an engrossing island of beauty and charm. Athena knew he would love a floating living treasure; she preferred the warmth and security of an island to leak terrifying memories that sunk within Agate's psyche, accompanies her own sad recollection. A small, inviting island, perceived catharsis, full of oozing beauty offered synergies to high tide, tie, their future together.

Ideal water worlds beneath and around them are teaming with alluring animals and organisms millions of years old. Athena pondered Agate's words as if they were a lifeline of prophecy: 'Eden' she related such words as sacred offering synergies of paradise rooted deep with the all-knowing of love, acceptance, without judgement. 'Perfection' No more. No less. A garden of Eden.

'Agate when I look out to sea, I see two wondrous worlds depicted 'As-One': The water-surface divides two beautiful worlds as an undulating curtain or membrane between; life above, and life below. Like one's Blood-Brain Barrier. You see...! When in that catatonic state I experienced, I saw the portals of life and so-called death ebbing and flowing, expanding like one's breathing chest? I am terrified at the thoughts of you frozen without me being by your side...

ACT Three
Silhouette Of Something Bobbing

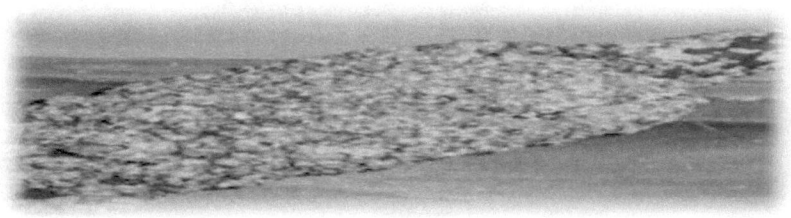

Etsy

'What are you looking at Athena'?

Athena's face pondered a meditative stare... something is drifting ever closer to them.

'I am looking out over there where the Sun is shining... I can see a silhouette of something bobbing up and down; can you see it, off to the left, coming our way, on the next wave break'.

Agate cupped his hands over his eyes.

'Yes, I can see it now. It is too deep for me to fetch'.

Athena stretched out her delicate hand, illuminating her shiny gold
bridal-ring that caught Agata approaching eyes. He attempts
to pirouette in-jest, spin around on one leg drilling himself into the
soft wet sand falling at his Angel's feet in a splash. In laughter,
Athena sings out laughing:

'Where every man should be... at the feet of their beloved.

Give me your hand my dear Crusoe...

ACT Four
Twilight-Till Dawn

*'Agate remember... you! Yes, you sent texts and pictures to me with your po-
ems. Hang on. I have got them on my phone... one minute; there you go, so far
were your words, reading them brought you closer to me when you were lost at
sea. A Special poem... our picturesque frozen moment in time. Let we read
some of it in stunned silence.*

Twilights Great Precursor
Our threshold of love hinged between the in-between.
Twilight-Till Dawn while at sea: Sung its lullaby; join our in-between.:
Twilight spoke the language of sunset, the silky moon
The Inbetween's whispered... I am Athena's shadow... in your shadow
of love I come.
Between we three...the language of sunrise, au revoir moon.
On icy ship decks, you work, while my shadow heart talks pillow talk,
companion thee.
Between we three...Twilight spoke the language of sunset... Bon
voyage silky moon.

ACT Five
Women's City, A Gift From God'

Captured Moments PDH

Approached their car, they slowed to a stroll taking in the beautiful surroundings gifting an aura of silhouettes as the evening nestled down. Another day of enlightenment was morphing around our two rare love birds. A rare mortal example of a true loving partnership; their veins awash with the most extraordinary blood group - AB-
...Coincidence!

'I am with you, my love...'

> 'What a magnificent spread of existence is dancing with colour, heavenly art in motion... It goes as far as Ones-Mind-Eye cares to focus, to ponder the impossible, to extrapolate this point in time into Stary beyond the beyond. To come back and give you my findings in one beautiful kiss that can only explain the impossible.'

'Agate, I love it when your Soul thrust your spirit travel: Every time you return, you give me a renewed kiss of life; We dock, locking our lips together, Agate you infiltrate, starts my inner Solar System: My Solar-Plexus; My Chakra; My 'Mani': Opens my jewel; My 'Pura': My women's city, a gift from God'.

> 'Athena, Don't we usually think and feel things intuitively;
> Outside of words and ACTion?'.

Yes, so true. Read, hear, sense each other thoughts, felt... part of our communication since children; in class. Remember walking home

from school playing 'what I am I thinking?' and, usually first thing in
the morning, whisperings.
Agate! Can you sense my thoughts I am sketching? A beautiful
goodbye to the sea, beach, sky and trees right now?'. Agate, can you
see Angels, not in the sky... where are they?'.

ACT Six
We Were Born To Love Each Other

Captured Moments PDH

Swoon with the high-spirited celebration, oozing excitement and
anticipation, Athena and Agate lowered the soft-top; through the
open windows, they sang along in refrain...to 'I was Born To Love
You'. Each breath finding harbour in each other's hearts; a silver
anchor within each soul. Hearts full, but feather-light, zooming in
love as the moonbeams through cedar branches projecting shadow
danced as they drove — high tide manoeuvring its creeping sounds
consuming the dampening sand with each ebb and flow.

'What Are you doing Athena... I am trying to put the light on... stop it
Athee; you better take a shower... Your so sticky; I need a cold drink'.

> 'We do not need the light on my love... perfect as it is, we have
> a room full of illusions with the sound effect outside, let us
> enjoy the moment as it is in its glorious perfection in every
> single way. Agate, we are not single anymore, married,
> bequeathed to each other without restriction orbiting each
> other's souls'.

ACT Seven
A Beautiful, Lively Aura

Captured Moments PDH

'Remain in love…

My childhood sweetheart Athena. My love grows stronger the older we become in life seminaries. Athena, from the time you open your dazzling coal-black eyes, I boil over wanting to float you away to a desert island just you and me. Sounding selfish… I speak how I feel. When you sleep, My jealousy rages at the Sandman. I chase your eyelids within my focused stare; A stowaway…to the land of Nod. Let me speak, let me share what I see beyond your slumbered body at rest while your spirit goes to school. I see a beautiful, lively aura, an offering that vibrates harmony of colour, an accord, with its pulse, a radiance that ripple hues and a song. Mixed with a palette of synchronised blues, greens and mauves charting up and down mostly northern osculating waves of light.'

ACT Eight
Something Inside Wanting Release

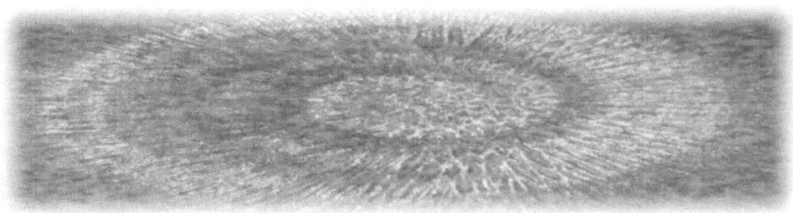

Captured Moments PDH

'What do you think about, Athena... loose change for your thoughts, my love, as it rattles in that beautiful cerebrum of yours?' SILENCE... A PAUSE...then...

'just admiring my war wounds from that old battle with the bottle we found. What did you do with it?'

'It's in my new backpack; I picked it up while you were daydreaming, looking out to sea. I hope it didn't leak. I ran out of time as all mere mortals do. I planned to check its seal when we got home.'

' Quiet now, Agate, all this talk of sands and time...I am hungry for seafood. How about you?'

'Let us guess what inside the bottle! Maybe a Genie... ooooh?'.

Athena side-glanced the bottle wondering... should I...? She didn't refuse. Bottled up was a magnetic command; to be touched and explored. Its content had an aura that was compelling, impossible to resist

ACT Nine
Experienced A Deep-Rooted Affinity Within

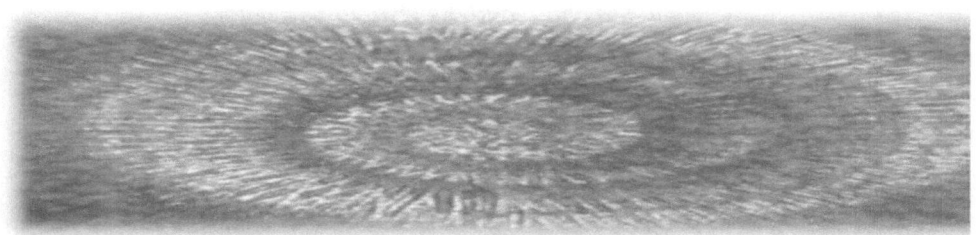

Captured Moments PDH

Agate opened his Swiss army knife and prepared to expose the camouflaged seal. He first chose the pliers to crunch then ground away from the hard barnacles followed by the use of the long, sharp, spearpoint blade revealing a glass orifice; preserved with a hardened sealing wax that fractured under the impact of the screwdriver. We exposed a large cork across the neck of the bottle. Designed to hold wine or any other hallucinogen readily available to all and varied. Agate delicately positioned the corkscrew's bevelled edge, entering the old stopper as it squealed like a stuck pig. Agate slowly calculated every twisting motion as the spiralling worm screwed itself more in-depth into the heart of the only matter that separated its contents from the earth's atmosphere. After the pig ceased its loud protestations and resistance to entry, it still refused to surrender its hold. Athena visualised the cork's stubbornness as a Coldstream-guard.

ACT Ten
We Still Have The Zebra Crossing... What Does This Mean?
Agate & Athena

'Agate, it is incredible: there is a life story in my hand wanting to stream forth as a cascading waterfall frozen in time; would you believe a biography crammed into not much more than a thousand words? A young woman, a child, and the vision I had before… Déjà vu.'

'Athena, my love, wait a minute… Athena, are you listening to me? ATHENA! Please look at me… put down the parchment and listen to me carefully… not hearing, are you?'

Unhearing or not, Athena pressed on, about to expose the saddest, yet most beautiful love story imaginable.

My psychometry will make contacts beyond the words written on the goat parchment. It's a writer's dream come true. We have discovered a long-buried treasure. Agate this is beyond imaging for me or anybody; you do not understand the trove within my hands… real happenings of the past made manifest after all these years in my hand to bring to life.

Moonlight still streamed through the partly open blinds as zebra crossings. Athena sipped on her tea as Agate drunk his chocolate admiring the silhouettes shadows of branches swaying in the sea breeze.

Agate, we still have the zebra crossing in our room?

Athena… What does that suppose to mean?

The computer screen flickered a few times as if being rocked, then stabilised

ACT Eleven
Athena Reads The Parchment
Agate & Athena

Bare Threads - An Amazing Tapestry To Behold

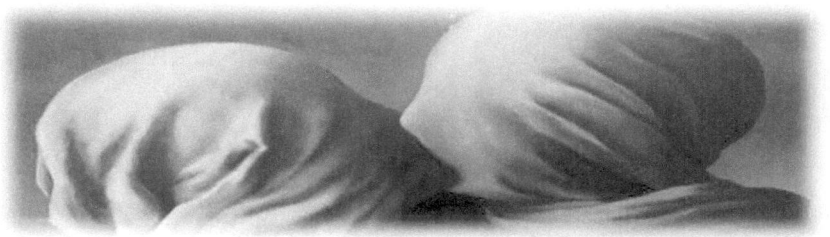

R. Magritte

'We wish you could hear us
Wherever you may be my love...'

I Knew I should have used them, my Silver Thread and Needle, that
hung between us, together with but parted us, unite... that night, you
held me tight.
Preserve my virtuosity; Maidenhead intact.
Your gun holstered, trigger cocked; my fate, held in your hand that
night of stars.
You always called me you're: 'Blessed Silver Threaded Needle'.

'We wish you could hear us
Wherever you may be my love...'

Holy sealed. Gaped enough to breathe its force: A cough, to sneeze
its forsaken monthly runs, eclipsed suns. Secured veil for none to see
nor touch but I... it's trusted, custodian until that starry night stare
with fright.

Grandmas, wise words vanished in mindless passion did we bear.
Salmons upstream did sporn grandma scorn. Should have stitched
engorged purse closed before your hypnotic kisses parted me so.
Somewhere unknown found its course.
Grandmas' warnings haunted me during unknown landscape read.

Was still... still, then his face distorts as if ill.
Then shot his gun... fired and found its mark.
A bonfire distilled within... spirit child from him, bottled within the
feminine crib.

'We wish you could hear us
Wherever you may be my love...'

Come blossom bud, dripped tears of fear and dread; Asked him:
'What have you done?'

Almighty God, I've succumbed in love... I shall pay the price of
forbidden love'.
Lovers busy bees love to seek nectar, fantasy safe course to go.
Eager nature stalks its prey. A girl's divine gift can be her curse.
She's a queen to hive her monthly bees. He wanted to love me; my
hive needed loving to be. I feared lied to. So, I did not ask him so... I
should have, this, I know. 'Do you love me? Honey don't sting me
then let me die alone'?

'We wish you could hear us
Wherever you may be my love...'

Fingers lay upon my Silver Threaded Needle. Other fingers unhinged
squeaky sacredness, opening the rusty-hinged door. A tune of love
unto others as you love them in your mind so.
Hung in the balance between Needle and Thread, grandma's words I
dreaded.
Honey, I kept you closed then opened. Between life and death.
Between love and loss.
Yes... No, no, let me go!
But the baby came his way; I stretched and screamed in unusual
ways. Wrong Thread slipped between my curtains; quivered as
salmon wriggled upstream into my Needle bed to spawn free to
grow, then part by crowning, another life, without drowning.

'We wish you could hear us
Wherever you may be my love...'

Welcomed your warmth inside me - As someone caught in blizzard
snow. Then, why did you run out of me in such haste and go? When

my lost chastity needed tender love to share bon voyage to my lost
virgin run.
Left freezing feeling wet, footprints in the snow to fret full of regret.

'We wish you could hear us
Wherever you may be my love...'

You left your port of call. I could scream ahoy no more. Breath
vanished as snow prints on my breast in a desert storm did its harm.
I released my arms; surrendered done.
Was I blinded by your lust, or was I blinded not to see, by the love
that consumed me hard and deep... for this, I would weep.
You deposited within me; before gushing out, floating love upon my
veil of blood.
Your charted course left my port... as if a storm was brooding mood
beguiled.
Part of you docked within my port! Your anchor left its mark, of
course.
A buoy lingered two days distilling; Cocktail mixed bleeding wonder
that indicted cultural thunder they might put me under before my
earthly time.

'We wish you could hear us
Wherever you may be my love...'

Upon the high seas, you sailed, in wonder, this I didn't know then.
You hovered between the horizon seas. Touching morning, evening
sky and sea without sharing my morning sickness.
My blighted condition offered flickering shadow pale light at night, till
morning sun.
A raging storm caused thunder in my heart and soul radiating out my
family rage. Lightning cast dark shadows to spook. Abandoned me,
you did; No money; No home, lost virtue, barefoot and impregnated,
fear of the unknown dawning mornings could not conceal my body
swell, a brewing storm intoxicated my loved ones, cursed me out.

'We wish you could hear us
Wherever you may be my love...'

Gazed times upon the silver Needle and Thread and wondered, what
if I stitched laced myself, boot-tight? But you would have squeeze
slipped past me when you kissed me that fatal goodnight. When said
with such passion;
"I'll be floating the seven seas for several months... I shall be back to
wed thee'.
I resentfulness imagined my maidenhead nail upon his masthead that
ventured, wayward bound, seaports to fish net virgin maidens. Gaff-
hook other holy crosses to bear... secrete their sacred veil to heel,
before heading off to sea in freedom.

'We wish you could hear us
Wherever you may be my love...'

They nailed Jesus upon the cross. His blood-soaked surroundings
give freedom by rebirth through loving forgiveness, love the enemies.
Spiritual emotions contrived my soul for our forgiveness. Conceived
feelings once; the notion being impregnated; I was no Madonna to
claim her mantle. Only bow and wash others feet to rest their souls
behold, in women, pain is a man's pleasure, how bitter and warped
I've become.

'We wish you could hear us
Wherever you may be my love...'

The final sentence set in stones for losing my sacred crown, and
family honour near aborted.
Replaced by thousand needled throned 'Condemnation's' daily per
week as I swelled.
Barbs spoke prickle reminders increased with my daily girth.

'We wish you could hear us
Wherever you may be my love...'

Secured our baby's life; gashed its way into being. Nine months to
leave the stage with age. Slipped its corded dock-yard into dry hands
cuddled tight. After opening broke anchor cord, birth tore. Grandma
used my sacred Silver Threaded Needle sewed me inside out. Allow a
pinpoint light for life to seep right.

'We wish you could hear us
Wherever you may be my love...'

Darling: your incessant chatting inside my head causes my moral
compass not to comprehend, but double-bend Your voice grows
more possessive, massive with the every-heart-beat of our child. I
now have love beyond imaging's artistry mother bonds with the
child.
Little fingers, little toes, smiling face that glows as it grows.
Your loud voice haunted me every sunset: visual reminders; audit
every day come nights I pray to suppress your words, but the truth is
not so. Forgive me once again, dear father. Wanting, your talk;

'Hello My Love'.
When I first heard you; I shouted out into the sailed fresh breeze:
'You left me as the humpback whale, a carcass left alive, I thought I
was going to die'.
Oil wick-lamp shinning out a beam of love, to welcome, rescue you,
from your ocean world homeward bound, for wife in waiting with a
child.

'We wish you could hear us
Wherever you may be my love...'

****
SUDDENLY AN OCEAN MIST WAVE ENTERS THE ROOM.
BABY RELEASED ITS MOTHER-BREAST, TO FEED ON THE
MIST.
BABY THEN STARED VACANTLY, WITH DEPTH... INTO
MOTHER'S EYES.
THEY BOTH   SMILED A DISTANT DELIGHT.
****
Echo loving words found portal ears... mother's hearts melted with
cheer.

My blessed Silver Threaded Needle,

'I beg you, my love, please hear my swelling prayer to offer thee'.

'Please forgive me, my' love! I was waving from the sea beyond
below, where no suns horizon, but an eternal sleep without a wake

to sail my spirit free awakes to an eternal slumber of despair.
I also was and remain captive. Within a wretched body, I call not my
home.

Seven days and seven nights before my soul was set loose by Gods
loving Angel found buoyancy of my soul from oceans depth to
surface. To face you and boy-child my loves.
In spirit dress: a cloud of mist; you inhale not as hail, but hallelujah in
the divine breath of love.

Left behind a Godly Star and Angelfish that delivered me sweet news
of our baby's birth.

My blessed Silver Threaded Needle I share my tapestry of affection,
my words weave, a portrait, us three... In amongst lavender and
honeybees sitting free.

You know not the truth of my enduring, endearing love; that never
sunk, much less capsized. For your balanced lance within my heart
that I use for oars, my rudders-stars guide.
I'm so sorry, forgive me please, I didn't say;
'Love you, my darling complete, offering my four chamber heart.'

My blessed Silver Threaded Needle.

When returning home to your loving arms; My final port to berth.
Catastrophe cast me a castaway to float a buoy in raging seas, a
hurricane drank our ship and me to sleep the eternal sleep.
My love for you: Your love for me was so high I could not enter
heaven's gates, although hell I expected to go.'
Holy spirit showed: delicate matters needed, the resurrection of the
soul not too late.
My bones now lay with creatures of deep my deserving.
Submerged with unimaginable sorrow and unquenchable regret
knowing;
A bastard of a man, was I leaving without giving you my charted heart
and soul a crime.
A bastard child they claim... that isn't true, A true husband and father
dead.

My blessed Silver Threaded Needle.

For I was returning home to you, my Silver Thread Needle, to our boy
child created in love. To build our haven right on rocks; together
grow old to slumber. To become our fruitful seeds within natures
soil, and sew love, as we daily toil. Not in doubt but expressed every
moonlit, moonless night.

My blessed Silver Threaded Needle.

Dreams I can only offer until your tomorrows-end, we reunite.
Dream messages; spirited from the other side
Dream whenever you think of me... those special lonely moments.
I'll be your second hand a new; with every pulsed thought consumed

My blessed Silver Threaded Needle.

My love listens carefully... very carefully now
'Remember the old Anastasia mosque, overlooking the green hill and
the Aegean Sea?

Seek my father's tombstone, engraved;
'Thimble Near The Sea'.
Follow the engraved words;
'...Seek, And Ye Shall Find...'
Your gold fortunes lie behind the emerald green tile
'Find'

****

Epilogue

Athena and Agate found the old crumbling Konak Mosque with a
Cemetery about ten miles south of İzmir Turkey.
Overlooking the green hills fashioned with three windswept trees
facing west overlooking the Aegean sea.

'Athena, I have found it... quick, over here.

Suddenly, Athena heard the words 'over hear'.
She closed her eyes instantly, hand cradling her stomach,
as she breaths out visualising her breath entering a void.
Opening her eyes, she senses being drawn, through accelerated
dawns, sunsets and yearly seasons, morphing into one celebration of
life.
In a fraction of a second; second represented years.
Agate secure Athena's hand as they enter a whirlpool of coloured
stars offering universal love...
Start of a new beginning.

Robyn Canning

I joined the Creative Writing class at the beginning of 2018 to gain some perspective into my writing skills from a group of peers. I have been writing poetry, children's stories and memoirs on and off since the age of eight. In my retirement I feel I'd like to explore writing more fully and perhaps attempt a novel.

The writing group is very supportive and has given me the confidence to write short stories which I haven't really done before. I have enjoyed this and it has given me the motivation to write more - which is important as practice helps to improve skills and broaden the experience of writing.

Going Home

Writing Exercise: "It had been ten years since I had been home
and didn't know what to expect."
Short Story

It had been ten years since Edmond had been home and he didn't know what to expect. As an angry sixteen year old, leaving his rural hamlet of Brendon in Devon had been an impulsive decision, fuelled by an explosive argument with his father and a lifetime of his verbal abuse, which had increased when his mother died ten years earlier.

Albert, Edmond's father, was caretaker of the Brendon School and church which included accommodation at the school house. To earn extra money to support his five children, he also worked at Hallslake Farm as a farm-hand. At age twelve Edmond had to leave school to work at the farm, enduring long hard physical days, always at the beck and call of his father and constant criticism. Sixteen years old and rebelling against his father's tyranny, Edmond made his stand and left, not returning until now.

Travelling by train from Paddington Station to Taunton, Edmond then walked and hitched rides along the rural roads lined with the familiar ancient hedgerows of stone and bush. A strange mixture of homesickness and sadness hit him unexpectedly as he passed the rural paddocks of wide open farmland, feelings that he hadn't experienced for many years. The hustle and bustle of working in London as a Barra boy and becoming a "Jack of all Trades"; two years in the Naval service during WW11 on destroyer ships and the chaos of war and indelible memories of that period, had left little time for thoughts of home and the unhappy family life he had left behind - that was better left in the deep recesses of his mind.

Rides were few and far between and fortunately one ride took him as far as Simonsbath in the highlands of Exmoor. Only 4 miles to Brendon and Edmond although tired felt a lightness in his step. As Edmond approached The Rockford Inn, nestled alongside the beautiful East Lyn River there appeared little change and he decided to have a quick pint before walking the final mile to the old Brendon School House. Edmond drank his pint quickly and moved on, now anxious to settle the anxiety he was starting to feel about returning home. As he rounded the final bend he spotted the old wooden gate, supported by the stone fence. Slowly moving into the yard, time stood still and he was flooded with memories of days gone by.

"Can I help you?" a tall slim man of about thirty asked.

"I'm looking for my father Albert, he's caretaker of the school house and lives here" replied Edmond.

"Oh he retired a couple of years ago and now lives at Alderford Cottage, the other side of Deercombe."

"Thanks" said Edmond. The thought of walking a further half mile slowed his step as he walked out the gate.

The cottage looked deserted. It was overgrown and badly in need of repair. He knocked, then heard a wracking cough. He entered and a thick haze of smoke filled his lungs and eyes. Himself coughing and eyes watering he entered what looked like a kitchen. A small Bodley stove was belching out smoke and in the corner was his father, bent over a table playing cards.

"What do you want?" a familiar although weaker voice than he remembered asked.

"Father, it's me, Edmond." There was only the slightest hesitation.

"Well, what do you want?" replied his father. Edmond spoke to his father with a confidence he didn't feel.

"I've come to see the family before I take a commission on the aircraft carrier Sydney and travel to Australia."

"Humph!" was all he got as Albert coughed and returned to his card game.

What had he expected - that time would heal past hurts? Perhaps, but that hadn't happened. Edmond took one last look at his father, knowing that trying to make conversation would fall on deaf ears. He slowly turned and as night was falling, trudged with a heavy heart back to the Rockford Inn, and a room for the night.

Bikies and Bingo

Writing Exercise: use the words 'bikies' and 'bingo'
Short Story

Jeanie was busy getting ready for her first day of playing Bingo. She carefully chose her favourite hand knitted lilac jumper and purple slacks - very comfortable for a couple of hours of sitting in what might be a drafty hall, on a cold winter's day.

Her life, in these some might call 'twilight years', was much as she had hoped, with one unhappy exception. She never thought she'd be going out and about by herself. Norm had always been the live-wire in their partnership and to see him languishing at home, unable to hold a conversation and tinker about in his shed each day, was heartbreaking. Strokes are soul destroying, and the stroke Norm had experienced had left him without speech and partially paralysed in one arm and leg. Depression had set in and was difficult to budge. Getting him to do anything was a monumental task.

When Norm had retired ten years ago, Jeanie being a homemaker, initially had found it difficult to have him 'underfoot' everyday. She wasn't used to having Norm dependent on her for not only the cooking and cleaning (which she had lovingly done all their years of marriage) but also constant company and what she thought would be an enjoyable stage in their life, soon turned into surprising boredom and frustration. It wasn't long before both Jeanie and Norm agreed they needed to find an outlet together outside of their home.

Jeanie set about searching for new activities and discovered the University of the Third Age in Whittlesea (their local area). The range of courses offered soon fulfilled both of their interests and they discovered a new world of friendships and acquaintances. Life was good! Then two years ago Norm had a stroke and life changed again dramatically. Jeanie now became a carer and at 73 years of age, she was feeling so much older than ever before. Exhaustion was ever present, and she found it difficult to keep positive.

A friend suggested setting up a roster of people to sit with Norm a couple of days a week, so Jeanie could get out for respite. At first she was reluctant, although being a practical woman she knew this was wise advice and eventually she approached Norm about the idea. He was ambivalent and didn't seem to care. For her own sanity she agreed, and some of their wonderful friends made time each week to sit for a few hours with Norm - something as it turned out seemed to brighten him slightly.

After being persuaded by her good friend Judy to try Bingo, Jeanie was excited to start this new adventure. She had looked up the rules and thought it seemed relatively straight forward and hopefully enjoyable as well as rewarding! Kissing Norm goodbye after settling Joe in for his catch up with Norm, Jeanie headed out for her 20 minute drive to the Epping Memorial Hall.

Within 10 minutes her usually reliable little car started to drift and she found it difficult to hold the steering wheel straight - *that didn't seem right,* Jeanie thought. She pulled over to the side of the road to take a look if she could see the problem. Tyres seemed okay and no problem was visible. She started the car and now found it too hard to turn her steering wheel towards to the road. *Must be something wrong with the steering*, she thought. As she fumbled through her bag to find her phone she realised she was trembling and anxious. Trying to sort her thoughts about what to do, as well as being concerned about either being late for Bingo, or more disappointing missing the session, Jeanie was aware of a dull hum in the distance getting louder and louder.

Looking in her rear vision mirror, Jeanie could see a procession of motorbikes moving at reasonable speed down the road behind her. The approaching noise became deafening, only adding to Jeanie's stress and she hoped they passed quickly so she could get on with her phone call for help. Several bikes passed by and then two stopped ahead of her car. *Oh dear, what do they want*, was her first reaction, *I hope they're friendly,* was her second, *maybe they can help*, was her third.

"Hello love, is everything alright?", asked a man, who Jeanie could only describe as a mountain. "Well no it isn't, but it will be if I can find my phone", replied Jeanie. "What seems to be the trouble, maybe we can help". "I think my steering has died, I can't seem to move the wheel", said Jeanie, who proceeded to open her door, after realising this was a friendly face, if not a gruff one. "Let me take a look," and with that the mountain of a man, in his worn leather jacket and dirty looking jeans, squeezed in behind the steering wheel, turned on the motor and gave it a try.

"Yep, looks like your steering rack is shot I'd say, it will need to be towed". Jeanie burst into tears. She couldn't understand why, but she chose that moment to have a mini breakdown! "Oh no, my first day at Bingo and I'm going to miss it" she cried. She found herself babbling on about Norm, how cruel life was and that she didn't think she could take much more - this wasn't Jeanie, but she couldn't seem to help herself.

Both men stood back, unused to people pouring out their emotions, they were a bit lost for words. "Where do you need to be love?" asked Tony - the mountain of a man. "Bingo in Epping, but I won't make it now" sobbed Jeanie, finally starting to compose herself. The men looked at each other. "We're heading in that direction, and we have a spare seat in John's sidecar, we can drop you there". Not really thinking straight, Jeanie replied "but what about my car?" "Lock it up and you can get it picked up after your Bingo game, you must have someone who can organise that haven't you?" said Tony taking charge of the situation. Time was getting away, and Epping was a bit further out of their way than he would have liked, but he couldn't leave this old dear alone to figure things out. "Well I suppose that would be okay if it's not too much trouble" said Jeanie, not really thinking anything through, her initial judgement clouded by her circumstances. "Right then, let's get your things and lock up the car". Tony handed Jeanie her coat, locked her car and escorted her to the huge machine that was to be her ride.

What have I agreed to Jeanie thought. *I can't go in that*, her thoughts almost bordering on panic. Holding Tony's arm she stepped into the sidecar. Her next thought was how comfortable the seat was and how similar to sitting in a car it felt. *Perhaps this won't be so bad*, she thought as she nestled into the seat. "All set love?" asked Tony. "Yes" replied Jeanie. With the beginnings of a smile on her face she looked up at Tony's laughing eyes. "That's better, think of the story you'll tell your friends!" The roar of the motor starting up unnerved Jeanie slightly, and then, surprisingly she felt a small thrill of excitement. *This is me having a motorbike ride. Won't my friends be surprised when I roll up in this! And, what a story to tell Norm tonight. I'll worry about my car tomorrow, hopefully it will still be there!*

The End

Poem: *Written in 1997*

The wizened form lay under the blankets
Still, so still, barely a breath.
Approaching anxiously, cautiously, what would I see?
Only a day or so and her life would cease.
Images of her beauty flashed through my mind
No longer there, her large eyes staring, ice blue, not moving.
Lips pursed, not moving.
Hands, clawed, skeletal, yet manicured nails.

Emotion welled.
Failing to stem my sadness, the tears flowed down my face.
An apology was trying to escape my lips and still my emotion
swelled.
Death, staring at me, frightened and resigned.
Voice no longer there, limbs no longer moving, only eyes staring,
tear filled,
unblinking saying so much wordlessly.

Her words of yesteryear haunted me.
"Better to be dead than like this."
Her wish would come true now, finally, the agony of living over.
I rejoiced for her, but sadness seeped into my soul.
Sorrow, despair, her last years a misery.
Body suspended still, yet living.
Brain active, but captured in a cocoon of stiffened muscle and tissue.

Not a fitting end for a beautiful lady of style and grace.
A cruel irony at the end.

✦★✲❧❧★✲✦

Last One Standing

Poem: Written in 2018

Another one gone, she thinks as she sits
Tired and sad at her loss
Her aching sore hands are clasped on her lap
As her mind tries to grasp fading time.
We can't escape it, we can't ignore it
Eventually it comes for us all,
A looming dark fog drifts in through the night
And your time here on earth is done.

She can't understand why she's the only one left
A pariah cast adrift in this life.
Unbearable loneliness, hollow and cold
Now her sister has passed and moved on.
How selfish and cruel, she thinks as she sits
To leave me alone by myself
I loved you too much, now the hurt fills my soul
And unspent tears tumble down.

Her eyes focus upwards taking in the room.
Voices somberley drift in and out.
She sees three generations all honouring her sister,
Supporting her with their wide open arms.
Whatever time she has left, they are her world
She isn't alone.
The new baby born this week,
 A gift to adore,
And the warmth of family gladens her heart.

Acknowledgements

Heartfelt thanks go to Whittlesea U3A for the support of this anthology of works. In two ways, for providing the infrastructure for conducting our Writers Group, and providing the resources enabling us to publish.

To Jan Marshall, valued Writers Group member and contributor to this anthology, for her hard work in formatting, compiling and preparing for publication.

To all of the Whittlesea U3A Writers Group members for their enthusiasm throughout the course of the year and for them making it fun to run, and their contributions to the anthology. A real team effort.

To anyone I may have missed thanks to all and all of the above for

Throwing Caution to the Wind

Whittlesea U3A

To find out more about Whittlesea U3A and the University of the Third Age movement, see https://whittleseau3a.org.au/

www.ingramcontent.com/pod-product-compliance
Lightning Source LLC
Chambersburg PA
CBHW020241130626
46549CB00005B/2008